M

Books by Pam G Howard

The McDragon Series
McDragon
Effel
McFinnia

Mr Spangle Series
Spangle

McFINNIA

PAM G HOWARD

Matador
9 Priory Business Park,
Wistow Road, Kibworth Beauchamp,
Leicestershire, LE8 0RX
Tel: 0116 279 2299
Email: books@troubador.co.uk
Web: www.troubador.co.uk/matador
Twitter: @matadorbooks

ISBN 978 1789018 479

British Library Cataloguing in Publication Data.
A catalogue record for this book is available from the British Library.

Printed and bound by CPI Group (UK) Ltd, Croydon, CR0 4YY
Typeset in 11pt Minion Pro by Troubador Publishing Ltd, Leicester, UK

Matador is an imprint of Troubador Publishing Ltd

For Alfie

CHAPTER ONE

The noise was horrendous, rather like fingernails being scraped down a blackboard. The woman on the footpath pointed her walking stick at the shrieking thing plunging down towards her and its fall slowed until it eventually landed on the grassy knoll beside her. There was an evil gleam of anger in her eyes as she again lifted the wooden stick – there was a flash and the gargoyle-like being next to her screamed as it was flung up into the air.

"You failed! Again!!" her shout was almost as piercing as the shriek of the squawkin.

* * *

The rain was sheeting down upon their heads as they trudged along the footpath to where they were staying. Although their anoraks were doing a great job in repelling the water, their trousers were soaked through from the top of their boots up to the edge of their coats.

"What do you think of this weather then Dragon boy?"

"Good weather for ducks is what my dad would say!" was Peter's answer to his friend Biffy.

They were on yet another school trip. It was spring and the powers that be had decided that North Wales was a good place for their geography field trip. They were to stay in a small hostel at the edge of a hamlet. Beautiful high mountains with white tops edged the skyline around them.

As they got closer to the hostel Peter felt a tiny warning prickle at the back of his neck, he turned to see whether Biffy had felt it as well, it was followed by the distant sound of screeching.

"That was odd, wasn't it, Dragon boy? That sound reminds me of the sound of a squawkin." A squawkin was an evil creature which had evolved from the gargoyles surrounding a wizard's castle in olden times.

"Me too! Along with the feeling of magic being used – dragon magic!"

"We'd best be on our guard then," Biffy puffed. "There always seems to be danger when dragons are involved!" He was beginning to look a bit red and sweaty. He was quite a chubby chap compared to his small skinny friend because he rather liked his food and, since he'd stowed away in Peter's dad's car when Peter and his dad were on a trip to the Isle of Harris in the Outer Hebrides, he'd developed a passion for cooking, particularly cakes, which didn't help his waistline at all.

The tingling feeling had passed, much to Peter's relief, but he wondered what on earth had caused it. He could hear the other boys who were with them chatting aimlessly around them indicating that the magic had not touched them in any way at all. Looking across at the nearby mountains the peak of one of them, rather oddly, turned pink. Strange, because it was nowhere near dusk.

The panting next to him was getting louder and Peter found himself slowing his pace down so that the two of them could continue to walk together.

They eventually stepped through the door of the hostel and Peter looked around him. It was quite basic, but at least they weren't in a tent this time. Mr Trubshaw, the geography teacher who was leading their party, quickly organised them into different rooms. Peter and Biffy were in a room with four other boys and the two lads immediately made a dash for two beds next to one another by the tall window. Not that anyone else wanted to be near them or would even consider fighting them for the best beds in the room. Biffy used to be the class bully and he and his gang had tormented Peter mercilessly over quite a long period of time until, Spit, Peter's young dragon friend, had blasted Biffy with dragon magic. Although Biffy had mellowed considerably over the last few months the other children had, understandably, long memories. Even Peter himself sometimes found it rather strange that he had grown to like Biffy despite the dreadful time he had had. He did have one niggling concern though, and that was on a few occasions he'd seen a couple of the old bully boys eyeing him strangely and he had this gut feeling that the bullying might start up again but with a different leader of the gang. Hopefully he was worrying about nothing.

They'd been told to hang their wet coats up in the bathroom on pegs which were lined up over a big, old fashioned bulky radiator.

When Peter changed into his dry trousers he made

sure he transferred his two dragon scales from the pocket of his damp jeans – he couldn't take any risks about losing them, they were what he used to chat to Spit, who lived in Scotland. All he had to do was to hold on to Spit's scale tightly and think of the little dragon and lo and behold they could see one another in their heads and chat as if on the telephone. Peter also had a second, bigger dragon scale, which belonged to the dragoness, Seraphina, and that worked the same way. Not that he talked to her as he did Spit – that scale was really for emergencies only.

Biffy nodded when he saw what Peter was doing, he too could speak to the dragons through the scales, but they had been given to Peter because he was the one who was deemed dragon kin by the dragons.

"Keep them safe, whatever you do, Peter!"

"Too right – I wouldn't want anyone else to get hold of them!"

Biffy had the grace to look a little guilty because when they'd been on their last school trip to Scotland he'd "borrowed" the smaller scale which had fascinated him – he wanted to try and understand what it was. That was before they'd become the unlikely friends that they were.

Peter rubbed the back of his neck again, "There's that feeling again!" he muttered to Biffy, "Did you see the way one of the mountain tops turned a red colour?"

"No, but I can feel that tingle too. What do you think it means?"

"I guess we'll find out in time, but as I'm not touching the dragon scales now it can't be to do with them."

"Let's go and find something to eat, I'm starving!" No surprises there.

CHAPTER TWO

The afternoon snack was cake and Biffy was very happy to hear that they'd be having supper later as well. He chuntered on and on to Peter about it, guessing what they might be having.

"Shame it's not going to be mussels with spaghetti like your dad cooks! Or haggis and neeps. I bet it's something like sausages and beans!"

"Well I happen to like bangers and mash."

"But you also like mussels or that nice mackerel we caught when we went fishing. That was lovely! Did I tell you that last week your mum showed me how to make lasagne and I'm going to try to do that when we get home?"

"How come you are always thinking of your stomach?"

"There's nothing wrong with liking my food. I might be a chef when I am older, I can't see me working in an office somehow."

Peter just smiled. Despite being so young, Biffy's talent for cooking was growing fast and he'd really got the hang of making cakes.

"I wonder what cakes they make here in Wales? It might be nice to learn how to make something that's traditionally Welsh seeing as I mastered a few Scottish recipes when we were in the Outer Hebrides."

The sun had begun to peak through the grey clouds and the rain had finally ceased as Mr Trubshaw told the boys that they could have the rest of the afternoon off and either explore or they could read in their rooms if they preferred but, tomorrow the school work would start, he added ominously.

Peter and Biffy decided to take the outdoors option. Biffy thought they might be able to see if there was a bakery nearby where he could get some ideas for different cakes and pies. Peter didn't like to tell him that it was rather late in the afternoon for bakers to have much on display, but he wanted to be in the open air so was happy to walk with Biffy down what passed as the high street.

The radiator had done its job and their coats and trousers were nicely dry. Biffy continued chuntering on about food as they walked through the village. It seemed that there was only one shop, and when Biffy peered through the window he was quite excited to see that at the back of it there were racks which must normally hold bread and cakes and various other goodies.

Peter wasn't that bothered so stared across to look at the high crags in the distance. Was it his imagination or could he see something rather large circling the peaks? He patted each of his coat pockets, but his binoculars must be in his bag. Drat! The back of his neck prickled.

The shop owner gave them a cheerful smile and came to the door when he saw Biffy staring in through the window to ask if there was anything he could help them with.

Biffy jumped straight in wanting to know about local delicacies and whether they were made on the premises. Mr Rees seemed quite thrilled to find someone who was interested and told him that if he cared to get up at 5.00 a.m. in the morning Biffy could come down and see what they were baking when he made bread, pies and cakes which were delivered to other villages in their van. He did add that Biffy had to get permission from the teacher.

"Just come through the side passage to the back door and knock. I'll hear you and let you in."

"Thank you! I'd love to do that!"

The boys ambled on their way.

"You'll have to go on your own to the shop, I don't fancy doing that, but I may get up early just to explore a bit on my own."

"OK, so long as you don't stray too far. Dragon kin you may be, but you still need to be careful."

Peter looked back at the mountains but whatever it was had disappeared.

They followed a small footpath which ran parallel with the back of the village. Biffy was soon puffing and out of breath again as it was quite a steep walk up the hill, and eventually he sat down on a boulder at the edge of the path saying he would wait there while Peter carried on. As a matter of fact, that suited Peter fine because before Biffy had become his mate he'd spent a lot of time on his own. This was really caused by his lack of friends because boys were scared off by the thought of Biffy and his gang bullying them if they hung around Peter. He ambled along for a while, enjoying being in the open air and looking at the lovely green scenery. The terrain was so different to the Isle of Harris, which had a wild and rocky kind of beauty. He looked up at the mountains and again felt sure he could see something rather large flying around the peaks.

Eventually, after a quick look at his watch he decided he'd better get back to Biffy who wouldn't want to be late for supper.

It was two tired boys who finally put their heads down on their pillows and fell asleep immediately. It had been a very long day.

CHAPTER THREE

Breakfast consisted of cornflakes and toast with jam or marmalade. Peter thought he'd best eat as much as possible to keep his energy levels up, but he couldn't quite manage the mammoth amount that Biffy put away. Biffy had decided the night before that he'd wait another day to visit the shop in the village.

They spent most of the lesson looking at the different rocks on the same hill that Peter and Biffy had climbed the day before. Peter found it quite interesting.

They broke for lunch and then had to write up what they'd studied that morning. Mr Trubshaw gave permission for anyone who had finished their written work to either go out or spend time in the small common room that passed as a lounge. It had a table tennis table in it so most of the boys opted for that.

Biffy wanted to read an old cookery book he'd found on the book shelves in the common room to see if it had any recipes in it which he could copy out and take home with him – Peter left him to it. He did remember the screeching yesterday and as a precaution told Biffy which direction he was going in set off in on his own up a different footpath out of the village.

Gentle sunshine warmed his face as he walked up the winding path. He rather thought it led in the direction of what he'd seen flying in the distance. Glancing at his watch he decided to speed up a bit because he had to get back for tea time, and he wanted to get as far as he could.

As he reached a plateau either side of the small pathway Peter's neck started to prickle gently again. He rubbed at the base of his head and continued to walk as briskly as he could towards where he could see the track narrowing ahead of him. The feeling became more insistent and he stopped to look around in case he could see what it was that was causing the sensation. As he did he felt a wind beginning to batter at him and staring above into the sky he was shocked to see a large red shape descending towards him. With an elegant bounce the big creature landed beside him on the plateau and lowered its long neck to peer into his face.

A voice boomed into his head, "Strange, I thought I could sense dragon kin. But you are not a dragon!"

"I may not be a dragon, but I am definitely dragon kin!" he replied as fiercely as he could while fumbling around in his pocket to see if he could grasp Seraphina's scale, but something was in the way and he couldn't get to it. He straightened himself up and began the dragon greeting hum and rather surprisingly the dragon relaxed slightly and joined in with his discordant sound.

When the greeting had finished the creature stared back at him, looking him up and down.

"How do you do?"

The dragon grunted a response, "What is the meaning of those words, dragon kin?"

"That is how we humans sometimes greet one another and it is how my friend, Spit and I first speak to each other."

"I am not a human!"

"I can see that but then neither is Spit. He is a Scottish dragon!"

"Hmmm… you know another dragon then?"

"Yes, in fact I have met six other dragons, four huge Scottish dragons and one younger one, who is my friend, along with a recently hatched dragonite. What's more, one of the dragons that I consider to be my friend is a dragon seer." He announced proudly. "I must say though that they are a little different to you."

"Well, of course! I am a Welsh dragon!" the dragon was silent for a moment as it continued to study him. Then, "Ridiculous as it is, I wished for some help and you have appeared, possibly because of that wish. Dragon magic can be quite odd sometimes."

The dragon's large face pushed up closer to stare at Peter as if trying to see into his head and then it whipped its head around and suddenly lifted off the ground calling, "She is coming! Meet me here tomorrow at this time dragon kin!" and as an afterthought, "I cannot believe that a human may be the only creature able to help me! And an English one at that!"

"I will do my best to be here!" Peter called as the tingle in his neck gradually dissipated. The dragon disappeared into the mists just as the feeling in the base of his neck restarted and he heard heavy footsteps marching up behind him.

A sturdy woman strode into the clearing swinging a walking stick in time with her feet as she moved. She was wearing a red cloak and had a black beret on her head. Her hair was twisted into a long plait and was very red, much like the colour of the dragon. Her eyes were sharp and piercing as she looked around her and came up to him.

"Were you speaking to yourself young man?" As she spoke he was fascinated by her nose which drooped at the end, much as the one he would have imagined the witch in the story Hansel and Gretel would have had.

"Yes… Yes." Peter stuttered back. "I was trying to remember something for the project at school." He just hoped his nose wouldn't grow with the outright lie. The thought made him smile as he imagined it drooping at the end just like hers.

The cloaked woman stopped immediately in front of him and sniffed in the air.

"Can you smell that?" she demanded.

Peter looked as innocent as he could and replied, "Pardon? I can't smell anything other than the damp mountain air."

She looked very closely and almost disbelievingly at him. "You cannot smell the animally smell? Something big has been here recently! Why are you on your own? Where are the other boys?"

"I like to get away by myself sometimes. It can be a bit overpowering being with other people all the time." He answered calmly, not like his heart which was pounding heavily.

"I see," she answered scanning all around her and then she almost pounced forward to stare intently at the ground just behind Peter.

"Hmm, are you sure you didn't see anything unusual close to this area?"

"Nothing ma'am. What kind of something were you thinking of?

"A very strange but rare large creature."

"I think I would have run if I'd seen something big." Peter announced quite politely. "Anyhow, I must get back now before they send out a search party for me. Goodbye. I hope you find what you're looking for." And with no more ado he set off back down the path pondering as he walked about how he was going to manage to get here at the same time tomorrow undetected.

He guessed she must have seen some sign of dragon talons marking the ground, which was a strange thought because dragons used their magic to remain hidden from humans.

* * *

When he pushed open the door to the hostel he discovered the other boys rushing down the staircase, so he knew it must be close to tea time. As soon as he'd hung his coat up he went down to see whether Biffy had saved him a place.

Biffy looked up at him gloomily as Peter sat down beside him.

"What's up Biffy? You look like something terrible has happened."

"It has! Just look at this cake, it's awful."

"Is that all that's bothering you?"

Biffy was pushing the piece of cake around his plate with a knife.

"See, it's not the right consistency, the air bubbles are not all the same and its quite hard to eat. Really, you'd think the cook here would know how to make a good sponge cake!"

Peter did his best not to giggle – he knew this was serious business to Biffy.

"Why don't you ask if you can make some cakes in the kitchen? They might let you."

"Brill! That's a great idea, I shall go and ask if I can do that tomorrow in our break!" and Biffy shoved his chair back and marched determinedly off in the direction of the kitchen. Peter just hoped that Biffy had the sense to be polite about the cake that he'd just started eating. He didn't think it was that bad, although he had to agree it was not as good as the ones his mum had made when they were on holiday on the Isle of Harris.

As soon as he thought of that magical Scottish island, it made him wonder about the red dragon. He was sure it was a she because she was a lot smaller than McDragon and even slighter than the lovely Seraphina. Peter wished he was in Harris waiting for the rocks on the small beach to melt away and reveal the huge black dragon and then they would fly together and talk about anything that Peter felt he needed to. He wondered what McDragon would make of the dragon he'd just met. He made up his mind to try and contact Spit later on using the dragon scale and Spit could talk to McDragon about it when he next saw him.

The door to the kitchen was flung open and Biffy almost bounced his way back to his seat. He slapped Peter on the back as he sat down, beaming from ear to ear.

"They're going to ask Mr Trubshaw if I can bake tomorrow after our lesson! Thanks for that Dragon boy! That gives me something to look forward to. Now, what shall I make? Victoria sponge, so they can see what one should really taste like? Or maybe some lardy cake or a fruit cake? I think my reading this evening has to be a cookery book!" he finally announced.

Peter raised his eyebrows up, as if Biffy ever read anything other than a cookery book recently if he could get away with it.

CHAPTER FOUR

Biffy was true to his word and spent most of the evening before they went to sleep studying a cookery book and muttering to himself. Peter was a little disappointed because there wasn't time to tell him about the red dragon. He'd decided he wouldn't talk to Spit or Seraphina about the dragon either until he knew what it was she needed help with.

The next day they spent an hour or two studying various rock formations and then went to a nearby lake to try out canoeing to help them let off a bit of steam. Peter spent a lot of time staring up at the distant peaks hoping for a glimpse of red in the distance or even a small tickle at the back of his neck, but there was nothing.

Having at last been dropped back at their lodgings they were told they would be allowed to have a break once their notes were written up after lunch and then they could choose their own pastime again. With a nod to Biffy, Peter set back off through the village to find the path he'd investigated the day before. He looked around him as he walked and was fascinated to see in one of the small front gardens someone had a stone gargoyle crouched down by the side of the front door. It looked rather like it was a sentry keeping guard with its tongue lolling out and a nasty look on its face, what's more it had wings sticking out of its back. Oddly his neck tickled a warning to him and he sped up to get past it as quickly as possible.

The prickle indicating magic nearby gave him a thought, perhaps he should pretend to go a different route from the one he took yesterday. He went past the shop which Biffy hadn't managed to get to yet for his lesson and began to walk up the footpath they'd both explored on the first day. There was a fork in the path that looked like it might go in the direction he really wanted to go so he checked behind him to make sure no-one was following and then changed route to run up the hill.

The swish of big wings above him was the only warning he had as he was suddenly snatched up and lifted into the air. He didn't even have time to utter a scream as a voice quietly told him to stay calm and not make a noise. He did as he was instructed but his whole body was tense because his instinct wanted him to fight off whatever had hold of him. He looked to see what was tightening around his waist and saw huge long talons were very firmly gripping him and at the end of the talons were tightly knit red scales.

"Relax!" the dragon told him firmly. "Look down over there, can you see her?"

And coming up fast from the village he could see the bright red cloak which covered the strange woman as she strode along thrusting out her walking stick in time with her steps.

"My magic is keeping her from seeing us, but she is very powerful. Let's hope she doesn't call on her demon to come after us."

"What d…demon?"

"That stone gargoyle near her house can wake up on her command. It has been searching for me for weeks now, that's why I need your help. Wait and I will explain all to you."

"B..but I mustn't go too far – I will need to get back!" then he thought about it, "Are we in dragon time by any chance?"

"Well done boy, yes we are. You must be used to flying with a dragon."

"I am, but not quite this way! I usually ride on McDragon's back."

"Ride on a dragon! Ridiculous! There is no way you can ride on a Welsh dragon's back, I certainly would not allow that!" she huffed proudly back at him.

Peter relaxed a bit, being in dragon time meant he could be away quite a long time and still get back for tea with no-one being any the wiser. He did wish though that he'd had time to tell Biffy that he was going to meet a dragon.

Her wings rhythmically plunged up and down faster and faster and Peter could see the distant tops of the snow-capped mountains getting closer. It was a great relief when, finally, he felt them descending to land on a wide ledge in front of a cavernous opening on the mountain. The dragon released him onto the rocky floor, which was freezing cold and he shivered uncontrollably as he staggered to his feet to stand before her.

"Ar…are y…you able to warm me please? McDragon used to heat me up before we flew." His teeth were chattering so badly that it was hard to speak.

She puffed herself up and then blew hot air gently at him and he gave a sigh of relief as he felt the heat go through him.

"I forgot you are just a human boy who gets cold easily," was about all the apology it looked like he was going to get.

"Thank you! It gets very cold up in the sky." He spoke politely. "Now how can I help you? Does dragon time affect that woman?"

"I am not sure about her. She is a bad person and her demon is evil. Its sound is horrifying too! Screeching enough to hurt!"

"When I was on the Isle of Harris the dragons called them squawkins. Apparently, they evolved from the gargoyles which were on a wizard's castle hundreds of years ago. Why does she send her demon after you?"

"Come with me and I will show you." And the red dragon spun around, nearly knocking him off his feet with her tail. He just managed to avoid it by jumping over the end like a skipping rope.

She went to the back of the cavern and there behind a rock was a tiny dragon, sound asleep. It was smaller than Popple, the young dragonite who had been inside Seraphina's Pearl (the name the dragons gave to a dragon egg) when she had hatched. Peter had managed to rescue the Pearl from the evil wizard, McMuran, with his dragon friend, Spit and his crow, Archie.

"Wow, a dragonite!" then he hesitated, not wanting to cause offence, "Rather unusual colours." The little dragon

19

was a luminescent grey but had a shiny silvery sheen across her tiny scales.

"She is indeed different because she is not a dragonite, she is a dragona and she is what the demon has been sent to find. The witch woman knows I have her, how I have no idea, but she does. She wants to steal her from me, but I cannot let that happen."

"Is she related to you?"

"No, she was given to me to keep safe."

"How did the woman track her? Is she a kind of wizard? By the way, the dragons on the Isle of Harris call me Petersmith, what shall I call you?" The questions spilled out of his mouth followed by even more filling his head.

"So very many questions and not enough time to answer them all! I shall call you Pedrsmith because Pedr is the Welsh version of Peter." Peter smiled at this and just nodded his appreciation as the dragoness drew herself up tall and told him her name was Brenda.

"How do you do, Brenda." Peter said formally at the same time as trying to stifle a laugh, how on earth did a fierce red dragon get a name like Brenda? She glared at him fiercely as if she knew he was trying not to giggle and smoke tendrils began to issue from her nostrils.

"How can I help you, err, Brenda?" and he almost snorted trying not to let the laugh escape.

CHAPTER FIVE

Snuggling down under his quilt, Peter pondered over the events of the day. He still hadn't had a chance to tell Biffy about it all because his friend had been too involved with the cakes he'd made and given out at tea time. All he could talk about was his time in the kitchen and the positive comments he had received from everyone when they had eaten the fruits of his labour.

Peter had managed to rush into the dining area just in time for tea time.

"You nearly didn't make it mate!" was all Biffy had to say to him crossly but for all that he still made sure Peter had more than one cake on his plate. The cakes were small sponges with butter icing on top. They were very light and tasted delicious.

"Smashing cakes Biffy!" was all he could splutter as he took another mouthful. At least he got a big grin in reply.

"I had to make them small or else they wouldn't have cooked and cooled in time for me to put the icing on top." Biffy's chest puffed out showing he was very pleased with himself. "I've never made such a big batch of them before, but I wanted to make sure everyone had some, although some people chose to have the fruit cake which the cook had made instead. No taste!" Then Biffy stood up explaining that he had to go and help tidy up in the kitchen before he started trying to catch up on writing the notes on the morning's lesson.

Peter knew he wouldn't have a moment to tell Biffy about Brenda in the morning because his friend planned on visiting the shop early the next morning to see what he could learn from the baker. He was going to be up at five o'clock, having first cleared it with the teachers and for that reason he disappeared off to bed early.

Peter went to sit outside, he didn't fancy joining the other boys in the common room and he was pretty sure they wouldn't be interested in him either. They had no idea that dragons really existed and would have laughed at him, much like Biffy and his cronies used to do. There was a wooden bench just outside which looked across the village and as he sat down he realised he could just spy the front of the cloaked woman's cottage. He was pondering over Brenda's problem when the woman strode past where he sat, swinging her walking stick in time with her marching and as she came abreast to him, she turned and looked at him nodding her head in recognition. He had to stop himself taking hold of one of the dragon scales just in case she could sense what precious cargo he had in his pocket.

Although he saw her enter her front garden and let herself into the cottage his dragon senses told him it could be dangerous if he tried to contact Seraphina or Spit, so he would have to wait until later.

Biffy was snoring loudly when Peter at last slipped under the bedclothes, wriggling about to get warm. How was he going to sleep with that racket going on and he got back out of bed and gave Biffy a prod. "Turn over and be quiet!" he told him fiercely. Fortunately, Biffy grunted and did as he was told, so silence reigned for the time being.

One of the other boys muttered, "Thank goodness, peace at last!"

Back in bed Peter reached across to the jeans which were lying next to the bed and pulled out Seraphina's big dragon scale. It warmed to his touch immediately and her calm voice echoed in his head.

"Petersmith! Do you need me?"

"Seraphina, I do need your advice please."

It was lucky that he was able to chat to the dragons through the scale without voicing his thoughts aloud, although sometimes he preferred to speak his words this was most definitely not the time to do that. It made him long to be on the island with the dragons when he saw the view from her eyes looking out to sea and watching Spit in the distance skimming along the top of the waves. He could almost hear the splash as Spit ducked down into the grey sea coming up very quickly with a huge fish in his maw. It was an idyllic sight, even though rain was pelting down there.

He told Seraphina of Brenda's plight and how the witch's demon, or what they knew as a small squawkin, was hunting Brenda and her small charge.

Adding as much as he knew about the dragona – asking if Seraphina knew what one was. She didn't, but she promised to question Effel or McDragon as soon as she saw them next. Her surprise was huge at the thought that Petersmith had now met and spoken to a Welsh dragon.

"They are usually very fierce and solitary," she told him. "Did she tell you the dragona's name?"

"Finnia."

"And did she tell you how you might be able to help her?"

"She wants me to take Finnia back home with me when I leave so she will be so far away that the witch cannot get her hands on her. I got the impression that Brenda considers Finnia to be something extra special."

There was a stunned silence for a while after that announcement.

Peter said it again. He really couldn't get his head round how he could manage such a task.

"A human, albeit dragon kin, looking after a dragon! My, oh my! Petersmith I need to give some thought to this. Brenda must be quite desperate if she is considering that course of action."

"I think she is Seraphina. She cannot fly her to safety herself because the demon seems to be able to keep track of her, so she needs to remain near to the mountain."

Peter yawned.

"Go now, Petersmith, I will need both McDragon's and Effel's thoughts on this strange course of events to see if they have some words of wisdom to give. Either Haribald d'Ness or I will fly immediately to the Isle of Harris to try to find McDragon."

* * *

The bell went to let all the boys know that they needed to get up and washed and downstairs for breakfast and Peter reluctantly dragged himself out of bed and off to the bathroom. He wasn't the only sluggard but luckily there was no queue when he got there.

They were already eating their breakfast when Biffy appeared in the doorway rubbing his eyes. He came over to sit down next to Peter.

"Was it good? Did you learn much?" Peter asked his friend.

"It was amazing, but I'm shattered now. I suppose if I decide to become a baker I'll have to always get up at that time in the morning. It was worth it though and what's more, I'm really stuffed as I've tasted a lot of what we baked. He said I could return tomorrow if I want to but I'm not so sure I'll have the energy to do that. I'll see how I feel."

"Well, we've only tomorrow morning and then we leave the next day. You could always go on the last day and sleep it off on the coach going home."

"That's a good plan! I hadn't thought of that. Did you enjoy your walk yesterday?"

"I need to talk to you about it. You may have some ideas to help me as I have a big problem to deal with…" and Peter lowered his voice and whispered in Biffy's ear, "dragons."

"Really." Biffy looked quite intrigued at this, "Okay let's try and speak after breakfast."

Peter nodded feeling thankful that Biffy was now aware there was a situation.

It was quite a while later when Peter and Biffy managed to get some time on their own and Peter reported everything that had happened to him in the last day or so. Biffy was astounded to hear about the witch woman who lived in the village.

"When do you go to meet Brenda?" Biffy sniggered as he said it because he too thought it was rather an odd name for a fierce dragon.

"This afternoon in the break but it would be good to have some sort of plan in mind before I go there."

"Hmm. Presumably Brenda will hand Finnia over to you at the plateau. The problem may be that the witch woman could well sense when you are around, seeing as you are dragon kin – that might be why she's turned up twice when you've been out walking."

"Good point! But you're not dragon kin and what's more even though you can sense magic it has no effect on you so it's possible she wouldn't be able to keep track of you if you came with me." The fact that magic didn't affect Biffy had made the difference when he'd had to help rescue Peter after he, Popple and McDragon had been captured by the nasty wizard, McMuran, in Scotland.

Biffy got quite animated at this point. "Yes, yes! I could take Finnia and carry her straight onto the coach."

"There's one thing though."

"What is it?"

"Finnia is a dragon, even though she is a little one and she will smell a bit. I wonder if there is some way that she could be sedated with magic and then sleep in my bag in the hold. I know it will be cold inside there but, she's used to that up in the mountains."

Gradually, the two boys began to formulate a plan which Peter was very keen to run past Seraphina as soon as possible. Biffy stayed close by while Peter tried to get in touch with the beautiful dragoness and he was so pleased when Seraphina answered him immediately, almost as if she had been waiting to hear from him.

She told him that Haribald had flown to the Isle of Harris, leaving Seraphina to oversee Spit and Popple. McDragon had not been in his rocky resting place and despite waiting, Haribald thought it best to return to the dragon's island in case there was more news. They did not know the whereabouts of Effel and could only hope that she would have a vision which would urge her to join the other dragons. Effel was a law unto herself and was impossible to track down.

Peter explained the idea that Biffy and he had hatched between them and they all agreed that it wasn't a bad plan, although it did have some holes in it. Apparently, Brenda should have the ability to put Finnia into a deep sleep, so long as Finnia did not fight against the dragon magic."

"My main problem, Seraphina, is when I get her home how am I going to feed her? What will she eat?"

"As a dragon she will be able to eat almost anything."

Peter had been communing with Seraphina out loud so that Biffy could hear at least Peter's part of the conversation when Biffy interrupted them, "Peter maybe she'd eat cat or dog food if necessary, that shouldn't be too expensive!"

Peter relayed this to Seraphina.

"I have no idea what humans consider dog food to be, but I would have thought that if an animal will eat it then a dragona surely will as well."

"Good. I think I have an old rabbit hutch to put Finnia in so she cannot stray which should keep her relatively safe. Do you think she'll be OK being restricted like that Seraphina?"

"You will need to ask Brenda to explain the whole plan to Finnia so that she understands what is to happen to her – you do not want a dragon, no matter how small not understanding why she is contained. Didn't you say you're coming to Harris again soon? If you are, bring her with you and we will keep her with us on the island."

"But again Seraphina, how will I keep her quiet in the boot of the car and what about the smell?"

"I don't understand what you consider a problem with the smell Petersmith. Dragons do not smell!"

"Well," Peter hesitated not wanting to cause offence, "it's like some humans smell different from others. It can depend on what they eat." He didn't like to say that dragons all smelled very different and their poo was very pungent indeed.

"Humrrph!" was the only answer Peter got. "If necessary we can send dragon magic through the dragon scales and aim it at Finnia."

"Cool!"

CHAPTER SIX

Biffy decided he would go along with Peter when he made his way up the footpath again and Peter was quite shocked when he glanced at the witch woman's cottage. It now had two gargoyles outside the front door!

"Wow, look at them!" Biffy nonchalantly walked over to take a closer look. Then had a shocked expression on his face, "I'm sure one of them winked at me!"

"Might have done," mumbled Peter, "this is the witch's house."

"Ah, that explains the feeling I have in my neck."

They carried on and before they turned the corner Biffy looked back at the house.

"Oh! Peter! There's only one gargoyle there now. Where's the other one gone?"

"We'd better hurry then, because that could be trouble for Brenda."

They strode on as fast as they could, Biffy's forehead beading with sweat. Fit he was not! He was panting heavily.

"Can we slow down a bit mate please? I've got to stop a moment and get my breath." And with that he bent over taking in gulping big breaths of air.

"Be quick about it, Biffy! We need to get out of sight as quickly as possible!"

"Ok! Ok!" and he straightened up and they set off again at a slightly slower pace.

As they rounded the next corner Peter stopped dead. There in front of them sitting comfortably on a flat rock was the witch. She too looked rather surprised. At the same time, Peter was aware of something speeding down towards them from the sky.

"Oh, you have a friend with you today!" she grimaced as she spoke and flicked the walking stick up making a strange sign in the air with it. Peter glanced up and saw whatever it was in the sky turn away and head back towards the village. It must have been the missing guard gargoyle!

"She couldn't have realised Biffy was with me," he thought. For some reason, not only could Biffy feel magic but not be affected by it, magic users couldn't sense him either. It was another good reason to have him around.

"He said I could do with some exercise," Biffy told her. "Not a great idea in my opinion but I thought I'd better go along with it."

The witch lady laughed and seemed to relax at that.

"Well, boys, I'll leave you to your exercise and head on back home. Enjoy your walk."

They watched her walk off down the path as Biffy pretended to bend over and get his breath.

"Is she out of sight now?" he whispered.

"Yes, I can see her red cloak down the bottom of the path. Are you ready to get going again?"

"Yup!"

"I can't see any sign of the squawkins, can you? The worrying thing is that now there are likely to be two!" They both peered up into the sky and Peter pulled his binoculars out of his pocket to scan the area more thoroughly. "I guess she thought that as you were with me I wasn't meeting a dragon or whatever she thought I would be doing."

"We need to keep an eye out for her though. She feels very odd and not in a nice way at all!"

"Yeah! I agree. She feels like McMuran did in Scotland and he was most definitely a bad un."

They slowed as soon as they reached the plateau and Peter checked back down the path to make sure they hadn't been followed and then he surveyed the sky for any spies up there. All he could see was a big shape with huge wings rushing towards them.

"Here she comes!" he warned Biffy.

Biffy, rather sensibly moved to the edge of the plateau to make sure there was enough room for the dragon to land, which she soon did.

"The witch woman was down there waiting for me." Peter immediately told her.

"I know, I saw her from afar and there was a demon above her. They've gone for the time being." Brenda looked sideways at Biffy.

"This is my friend Biffy. He is going to help us. He was amazing when I was kidnapped by a wizard in Scotland. It was because of him that I was rescued. He can sense magic but not be affected by it."

That made Biffy look a little embarrassed. "Wasn't just me you know, Effel was there as well!"

Brenda interrupted them. "So, you've decided to help me, Pedrsmith?"

"Well, we have a kind of plan and I ran it past Seraphina, the dragonness in Scotland and she agrees it may well work. It just depends if you are able to put Finnia to sleep so she can travel in the luggage area of the coach."

"Of course, my magic can do that!" The dragon sounded offended.

Biffy kept watch down the path and up in the sky to make sure all was well until at long last Peter had gone through everything and Brenda lifted her head and stared into Peter's eyes.

"Pedrsmith, it would be perfect if the dragons will take care of Finnia once you get her to Scotland. Finnia is of great importance. You will need to make sure that the Scottish dragons magically cloak her for the trip to the Isle of Harris making her drowsy so that she can travel in the boot of your father's car, much as I will do for her trip in the school coach. It will need the magic of more than one dragon to do that from afar and I could not manage it on my own."

The boys both nodded seriously at her.

"The dangerous bit is when I pass her over to you. The witch woman or her demon could interfere and take her from you. That is the very worrying part of the escape plan."

"Biffy will take her, because magic does not affect him and that will help keep her safe."

"Good. Good."

"But, Br…renda, you need to be very careful as there are now two demons."

The big red dragon put her head on one side as she heard what Peter said.

"Two, you say. That is very worrying!"

"Br...Brenda?" he spluttered as he bit his lip to stop a snigger coming out, "can I ask where did Finnia come from?"

"Pedrsmith, that is for her to explain, although I do not believe she is aware of the full story and neither am I. However, when she is with you, you must guard her in every way you can, but, be aware that Finnia has her own thoughts on matters and she is beholden to no-one, be they human or dragon!"

The boys looked at her hopefully, but she did not add anything more.

"How can we let you know that Finnia is safe? I can talk to Seraphina through a dragon scale from her chest."

Brenda looked quite affronted at that, "I will not give you a dragon scale. Can you sing?"

"Pardon?"

"We Welsh dragons are very musical. If you can sing out loud in the open air so long as there is a breeze, then your song will reverberate up to the clouds and will reach me. It is a very special sort of magic which only Welsh dragons have. I will need to put a tiny seed of that magic into you for it to work."

"My singing is worse than my humming, mum says I'm tone deaf and out of key."

"You can't sing!"

"It's never mattered before."

Biffy interrupted them by bursting into song. Peter was absolutely stunned because his rather plump friend had a gorgeous melodious voice. It was so lovely that the tension seemed to drop from Brenda as she relaxed with it.

"That is so soothing! You must have Welsh blood in you!"

"I don't think so, you know other nationalities can sing just as well!" Biffy responded looking rather embarrassed.

"There's a problem though Biffy." Peter said.

"What's that?"

"Brenda will not be able to sense you due to the fact that you are non-magical." The two boys and the dragoness pondered for a while on this problem.

"How about if Peter sings along with me, will your magic in him carry our voices on the wind to you?"

"I will fly high above you and we will try, but before I do I need to touch you with my dragon magic." She touched her snout to Peter's forehead and then, just in case it might work, pressed on Biffy's too.

"You are correct young human, I can feel nothing in you. Nothing at all." With a big rush of her wings she lifted up into the air until she was a speck above them.

Peter looked very uncomfortable and stared at the ground. He was not going to enjoy this at all.

They waited a while and then Biffy started to sing Land of Hope and Glory looking as if he was relishing the opportunity to sing out loud. He shoved an elbow into Peter's side and nodded fiercely at him. Peter rather hesitantly joined in and even Biffy winced at the flat notes which were coming out of Peter's mouth.

It wasn't long before Brenda plunged down to land next to them.

She looked at Peter, "You are quite correct your singing is truly terrible! You cannot have any Welsh blood in you!"

"I did warn you."

"Strangely, Biffy's music carried to me, there must be something different about him when he sings, and I will be able to tell when it is the two of you because of the awful noise that you make Pedrsmith. Remember when you want to let me know all is well, make sure you sing when there is a breeze, that is all my magic will need. Sing that music together when it is good news, but if there is a problem just you, Pedrsmith, sing out loud and I will be warned."

"How will we know that you have heard us?"

"Trust me young man! When you have finished your song look upwards and you will see a sign which will be very clear."

The boys watched Brenda take off again, very elegantly.

"Nothing like Effel's flying is it?" Biffy snorted as he laughed watching the red dragon fly towards the distant mountains.

"Look!" he elbowed Peter hard in the side, "They are after her!" As soon as the words left his mouth they heard the sound of a walking stick hitting the ground rhythmically and the red cloaked witch woman marched towards them.

"Don't look up, whatever you do!" Peter said taking his eyes from the dragon which was now being chased by two small black dots.

"Good afternoon," they chorused politely to the woman, just as a loud screech echoed across the valley.

"What on earth was that!" Biffy said, knowing full well it would be the sound of a squawkin which had been attacked by a dragon. "I've not heard a bird like that before!"

The woman smiled, her droopy nose wobbling at the end, "We have some rather different large raptors in the area," she answered.

"Oh, I'll have to look them up when we get home," Peter grinned back at her. "I like birds. Do you know what they're called? Oh, there it is again!" and he tipped his head to one side pretending he needed to listen intently, the screech, although distant hurt his ears, "Shame, it seems to have gone quiet now."

"Indeed, it certainly does. Unfortunately, I have no idea what it's called, so I can't give you a name to look up."

Peter was just thinking that her nose must be the length it was because of the times she must have lied when Biffy interrupted and said that they needed to be back at their lodgings or they'd miss tea.

"Goodbye, we probably won't meet again," Peter told the witch, "we go home tomorrow."

As they walked back he suddenly had a thought, "Oh drat! I should have offered Brenda to speak to Seraphina through the dragon scale! Stupid not to have given it a thought until now!"

"You can't think of everything, Dragon boy. We'll manage somehow!"

CHAPTER SEVEN

It was good to wake up on their last morning and know they were leaving but they were both very nervous. Would their plan work? The rescue would be fraught with danger.

Biffy had set off early in the morning to have a final session over at the shop, but he promised to be back in time for breakfast. As soon as they were packed they would meet with Brenda and her charge at the plateau. The boys were going to ensure there was room in one of the bags for the tiny dragon and they would also wrap her up in a towel so that if she did wake too early, she would remain safely in place.

A rather tired looking Biffy came into the dining area just as breakfast was over.

"Lucky I'm not hungry!" he announced looking at the clean plates all around.

Packing finished they set off through the village both feeling a bit scared about the task ahead of them.

"Peter, look! Where are the gargoyles?"

Peter checked and was shocked to see that neither of the gargoyles were in sight.

"Oh dear! That doesn't bode well for us, does it?" He checked the grey skies above them but apart from heavy dark clouds which were gathering there was nothing to be seen so it was quite likely that their last morning in Wales might be like their first one, very wet.

Peter felt the tension running through his whole body. The whole plan might be doomed from the start if the gargoyles were out hunting already.

"We'd best be on our guard from now on Biffy. Goodness knows what on earth is going to happen but remember, keep out of reach of any gargoyle talons. Although they're small if they're anything like the squawkins in Scotland, according to McDragon, a mere touch can kill a human instantly and although these gargoyles don't seem to have developed quite the same way, they could be equally as dangerous."

The boys moved up the path as fast as they could, constantly looking either side of them and up into the sky.

"I have a tickle at the back of my neck, so something is around! Can you feel it Biffy?"

"Yup. I'm scared! I'm not as brave as you."

"Don't you believe it mate. I'm petrified myself."

As they neared the plateau Biffy pointed out towards the mountains in the distance.

"What's that over there?"

Peter pulled his binoculars out of his pocket and stared through them.

"I think it's Brenda!" he turned in a neat circle to scan the area all around them. "She's heading this way! But what's that?"

There was a brief silence as Peter stared at what was following Brenda.

"Oh no! I can see one of those pesky squawkins some distance behind her! Has she seen it? How can we warn her?"

"Sing! Sing Peter! Now!" Biffy ordered. "Just do it! Give me the binoculars so I can watch what's happening."

Peter's voice crackled out discordantly into the air – it was a horrible noise.

"Louder! Make it louder!"

The sound seemed to reverberate around them and Biffy gave a running commentary of what he was watching at the same time.

"She must have heard because she's changed her course and is zigzagging about. I think you can stop now! In fact, please stop! It's hurting my ears." It would have been funny under different circumstances because Biffy sounded quite serious, but this was no laughing matter and Peter stopped immediately.

"Thank you!" Biffy breathed.

"I think we need to run up to the plateau. Is she getting any closer?"

"Yeah! She's heading this way fast in a roundabout route."

They sprinted up the hill but just before they rounded the corner Peter stopped dead in his tracks.

"She's there! The witch is sitting on that flat rock in the plateau. What shall we do?"

Brenda was racing towards them, faster and faster with a gargoyle close on her tail.

"Biffy! You go down the track a bit and I'll keep going as a diversion. Once I'm out of sight you sing as if your heart is going to burst. Let's hope Brenda understands to come to you to hand Finnia over and then you run down the hill. I'll follow as soon as I can. Get ready!"

Biffy gave Peter a pat on the shoulder, and then he turned and shuffled back down the hill they had just come up.

"Good luck Dragon boy!"

Peter braced himself and as soon as he heard Biffy's dulcet singing he marched around the corner to face the witch woman.

She smiled evilly at him as he came into view.

"I thought you would come this morning boyo. I've been waiting for you! Is that your fat friend singing? He's rather good even though he's not Welsh."

As she said that one of the gargoyles came into view about to land near her but on spotting Peter it sped away. It had been close enough for him to see its evil eyes were full of malice. Peter could see the other one not too far away, still trying to catch up with Brenda.

"I...I wanted one last look at the...the mountains. That's why I'm here." He stuttered. "It's quite beautiful and I don't think we'll be returning to this area again at any time in the future."

Brenda flashed past unnoticed behind the witch, diving down towards where Biffy was, out of sight from the plateau. The musical voice stopped and only a moment later there was Brenda soaring upwards again, dipping and diving to avoid a flying gargoyle near her tail. She slashed her long tail and with a scream the squawkin dropped from the sky.

"There's that weird sound again! Did you hear it?" Peter asked politely hoping to keep the witch woman's attention on him. She flicked her hand in the air and a second gargoyle joined in the chase. At that very same moment there was a rumble of thunder followed immediately by a flicker of lightening. The thunder was so loud that it took both the witch woman and Peter totally by surprise.

"I must go before I get too wet to get on the coach!" Peter called across the plateau and spun round to hare off down the path towards the village. He didn't stop to see if she was following him, but he was very pleased to see there was no sign of Biffy when he turned the corner.

CHAPTER EIGHT

It was two very relieved boys who sat next to one another on the coach. Biffy nodded at Peter as he sat down next to him.

"It's good when a plan goes right!" he said looking very pleased with himself.

The heavens had opened, and torrential rain was pounding down onto the ground so hard that it just bounced straight back up. Peter sped past the witch's cottage towards the boarding house where he could see other boys clambering on board the coach parked as close as it could to the main door. The boys hunched down into their coats trying to stay as dry as they could. Peter launched himself straight onto the bottom step of the coach and looked around for Biffy letting out a sigh as he spotted the big boy sitting quite near the front with his head resting against the rain splattered window

The coach's engine rumbled and started to tick over as the driver got ready for the off.

"Did you get the package OK?" Peter asked quietly.

"Yes, all settled comfortably in the bag and I loaded both mine and yours last just to make sure there weren't any other cases bundled on top of them. Lucky that we'd thought of that."

"Too right! Let's hope we leave straight away."

A rather wet Mr Trubshaw clambered up the steps to stand at the front of the coach counting boys and Peter's heart sank into his boots as the man cleared his throat loudly to get everyone's attention and held up a pair of crumpled stripy blue and red pyjama bottoms in the air.

"Who is the proud owner of these?" he called down the coach to resounding silence. Peter was panicking inside. They needed to leave now! He looked at Biffy who also had a very worried grimace on his face. The pyjamas were waved about in the air and at long last one of the boys put up his hand to claim them.

"I hope no other boy has forgotten to pack something!" Mr Trubshaw thundered at them. "You were told to check you had everything and particularly to look under the beds."

Biffy gave Peter a quiet nudge, "Over there!" and he indicated with his head towards the witch's cottage just as a dripping wet gargoyle shot past the coach to land beside the front door. It looked rather wobbly so maybe Brenda had managed to slap it with her tail.

"I hope we can leave now before the witch arrives in case she sends them after us!" Peter whispered, "Come on… come on!" He was feeling rather sick and was quivering with worry.

Mr Trubshaw turned to speak to the other teacher briefly to check on numbers and then told the driver to get going. The door unfolded and shut with a bang and the big windscreen wipers screeched across the glass, battling to clear the heavy rain out of the way.

As they rattled off down the road Peter was very relieved to see there was still no sign of the witch.

"Maybe she's on the plateau keeping an eye on the other squawkin," Peter said quietly. "I hope Brenda is leading it a merry dance to give us time to leave! This bad weather may help us."

Biffy yawned. "I certainly hope so! I'm exhausted and need to have a nap." And almost before he had finished speaking his eyes had closed and he started to snore.

* * *

Biffy slept for most of the journey until when they were only a few miles from home Peter nudged him awake.

"Is it lunch time?" were the first words out of Biffy's mouth.

"You slept through lunch."

"What?! Never!!"

"I tried to wake you but you just mumbled something and carried on dreaming. Don't worry though, I kept some sandwiches for you."

"Thanks, matey! Can I have them now please? My stomach doesn't like being empty."

"I noticed!" was the answer as the packet of sandwiches were passed over and opened by a podgy hand. Inside were egg mayonnaise sandwiches and the smell reminded Peter of the ones his mum usually made to eat on their journey to the Isle of Harris. Although they smelled very eggy, they certainly didn't taste as nice as the homemade ones.

As Biffy chewed away on his rather squashed lunch, Peter wondered how Finnia was getting on. Was she still in her magical doze? They had yet to get her safely inside Peter's house and then he needed to pull the old rabbit hutch out of the shed and set up the run before anyone else arrived home. He had a vague feeling that there was also a sack of old wood shavings somewhere about which he could use. What was concerning him was that she'd been asleep the only time he'd seen her, and she didn't know him at all. He could only hope that Brenda had told him about Pedrsmith. Nothing they could do about that now.

"Will you be able to help me sort out the stuff in the shed for Finnia, when we get home?"

"I would think so. My parents should still be at work – not that they'd care whether I was home or not. What about yours?"

"Should be at work as well. It'll be a problem if they're not because I'm not sure what they'd think of me going straight down to the shed when I haven't been in there for months and months. It used to be my den so hopefully I can resurrect that idea and that should keep everyone, including Alice out of the way."

"I'd best go home first and then come over, if that's OK with you?"

"Yup. Come down the back alley and I'll unlock the gate ready for you. It's a dark blue one so you can't miss it." Then as an afterthought, "I take it she's in my bag not yours?"

"Yes, I thought it made more sense that way." Biffy pushed the last bit of his sandwich into his mouth and chewed away thoughtfully.

"Not bad these sandwiches, but the bread could do with a little more flavour in it." Peter laughed and raised his eyebrows up. Biffy and his stomach!

* * *

The relief that Peter felt when he let himself in the front door was quite something – thank goodness no-one else was in and it was a little too early for Alice to come out of school as well. They'd been dropped at the school gates and as no-one was there to meet him he'd walked home carrying his bag – swopping it from one hand to the other when it got too heavy. He hadn't realised he was so concerned about his homecoming. He was also very pleased that the rain had finally relented, allowing the sun to peep though the clouds. There was a faint rainbow which looked like one end dropped down behind the roof of his house. It reminded him of the rainbow which Effel had magically moved to summon him to meet with her the first time.

He lugged his bag up the stairs and put it carefully down onto his bed to unzip it. A snoozing Finnia looking quite comfortable still wrapped in a towel. He lifted her out gently and sniffed. Not bad – she didn't smell too strongly of dragon which was another thing to be pleased about. He opened the window just to make sure that no odours remained behind, although if there were any complaints from his mum, he would say some of his things had got wet and hope that covered the subject. It was the truth.

After rummaging through his belongings, he shoved most of them into the washing bin and then clutching the little being against his chest, ran down the stairs and unlocked the back door.

Placing her gently on a shelf by the door, he found it was very satisfying pulling bits and pieces out of the small shed and remembering when they had last been used and it wasn't long before he came across the rabbit hutch. It appeared to be in good shape only needing a brushing to get rid of all the dust. He used a garden rake and moved the brambles that were growing behind the shed aside. He didn't want to get rid of them, only make room for the hutch underneath and then he pulled the weeds back over it to keep it hidden. The run fitted nicely behind the small gap between the fence and the shed and Peter was quite satisfied with his handiwork when he stepped back to admire it.

Throughout his labours he kept checking on Finnia but she'd continued in her magical slumbers and eventually he lined the hutch with the wood chippings, which he was delighted to find weren't damp at all. Just as he filled the water bottle with water which had been used for the last pet he'd had in the cage he heard the click of the back gate as it swung open.

Biffy stepped through.

"You took your time! I've nearly finished." Biffy squeezed himself through the gap behind the shed.

"You seem to have thought of everything, but I have the last and maybe one of the most important things here!" he announced proudly and unzipping his bomber jacket, pulled something out and handed it to Peter.

"Very mysterious," Peter said as he unwrapped the package. "Oh… that's great, food for Finnia when she wakes up!"

"Well, mum won't be suspicious when she finds it gone. She knows I'm always hungry."

"Naturally!" Peter answered, smilingly. "I never gave it a thought but, of course, Finnia will want food when she wakes up! I think there's an old bowl in the shed. I'll just get it."

The contents of the package were emptied into the newly washed bowl and it was placed reverently into one end of the rabbit hutch by Biffy. He had cut up some cooked beef into tiny cubes which were the perfect size for a small dragon's jaw.

They both bent over the tiny thing. She was so small and looked so delicate.

"Wow! She's rather beautiful, isn't she? Hard to think that she's a fierce dragon!"

"Well, Brenda wasn't as big as the Harris dragons but for all that I definitely wouldn't want to meet her on a bad day!"

"Neither would I! Let's hope Finnia realises that we're friend not foe."

They stared with awe at the small dragon that lay in Peter's hands. She felt cold to touch and it was a relief to see her tiny chest moving up and down. Neither of them would have wanted to explain to Brenda if she'd died in the bowels of the coach.

"Look at the tiny scales that cover her body, the pattern on them is so intricate and her colour is amazing!"

"I suppose we really ought to put her in her new temporary home." Peter suggested. "It doesn't seem right though, a dragon living in a rabbit hutch."

"Well, that's better than being taken by the witch woman."

"Too right! That's a good way of looking at it!"

She fitted perfectly inside the bedding area and when she woke she could wander through to the other side and munch at the food and suck water from the spout on the bottle which was fitted to the mesh of the cage. A small ramp led down to the run.

"Excellent!" the boys announced together.

CHAPTER NINE

Over supper that evening Peter nonchalantly announced that he was going to resurrect his den in the shed.

"That's a good idea, Peter. What made you think of that?"

"Well, I thought it might be nice if Biffy and I could use it. You don't mind do you dad? We'll start sorting through all my stuff in there to make more room."

"I'll be more than happy to see it put to good use lad. When will you begin?"

"Tomorrow, I think, seeing as it's a Saturday – I realise it's very close to us travelling to Harris but I can make a start at least. Biffy will help once he's made some cakes at home from a recipe that he wants to try out."

"That boy does enjoy his cooking, doesn't he?"

"Oh yes! I think that's an understatement!" and Peter went on to tell them how Biffy had made the cakes for tea one day while they were on their trip and about his early morning sorties to the shop in the village to learn how to cook local delicacies. That made them all chuckle.

"Well, I hope he's going to bring something yummy for us when he comes tomorrow." Alice chipped in.

* * *

The noise in the night woke him up from a deep sleep. It was a very unusual sound – very sad. He sat up in bed and listened as it set one of the dogs that lived nearby off and made it howl. Peter leapt out of bed and grabbed his dressing gown and slippers and then padded quietly down the stairs, making sure that he avoided the creaky one.

"How is it that all staircases appear to have at least one creaky step?" he thought to himself.

The back door squeaked as he opened it and he hesitated for a moment. No-one else in the house stirred so he carried on and once outside, ran down the garden path to the shed.

There it was again. As he thought, it was Finnia.

There was enough light from the moon above for him to see where she was lying pressed against the side of the rabbit run. Once he got there she just gazed up at him soulfully.

"Oh, Finnia! Why are you so sad? Didn't Brenda explain to you what was going to happen?"

He could have sworn that a tear slipped down her tiny face.

"OK. Just wait a moment."

Peter pulled one of the stakes that was holding the rabbit run down and lifted the whole thing up. Then he reached down and lifted her into his arms. She snuggled down against him just like a baby, or a puppy.

The dog that had been barking finally quietened.

"Do you want to stay with me tonight? Will you do what I tell you?"

The little dragon nodded. It was good that she seemed able to understand him.

"Alright, I'll take you with me."

As he started to turn he had a thought and looked back to check if any of the food had gone.

It hadn't been touched, so holding her tightly with his hand that only had two fingers and a thumb on it, he bent down and unlocked the hutch door and pulled out the bowl of meat. He also had the forethought to take the water bottle with him, just in case.

"There's one thing though Finnia… and please nod to let me know you understand this… if you need to pee you have to let me know so I can bring you outside. My mum would go mad if you did it on the carpet and you really don't want that to happen, I can promise you that!"

The little dragon must have understood because she nodded again.

Back in his bedroom Peter offered her some of the water and she drank greedily and then gobbled up most of the meat as if she was half starved.

Having taken off his dressing gown and hung it up he clambered back into bed and was amused when she snuggled in against him closing her eyes immediately. His last thought before he dropped off to sleep was that Brenda would not approve of a dragon, be it Welsh or Scottish, wanting to sleep next to a human in bed.

The following morning went quite well, all things considered. As soon as he was up and dressed he took Finnia outside behind the shed to relieve herself. Then he offered her some more meat and water and said she had to stay in the rabbit hutch while he went to see his mum and dad and that he'd be out as soon as he could. Finnia made it very, very clear that she was not going to be put back in the hutch again and in the end all he could do was to take her back into the bedroom and hide her under the bedclothes. She nodded her agreement to stay there until he came back.

It concerned him a little because it was fine while he was at home but what could he do with her when he went to school? He'd have to think on that one and come up with an answer.

Breakfast with his parents was quite rushed because they both had jobs they wanted to do and what's more Peter and Alice had to carry out some chores as well.

Peter kept checking on his watch while he cleaned the bathroom. He made sure he did a good job of it because experience had taught him that he'd be sent to do it all over again if he didn't. Every now and then he'd slip into the bedroom to make sure Finnia was behaving herself and it was a relief to notice that there was no aroma of dragon in there at all and certainly no signs of dragon poo either.

When Biffy eventually turned up he was clutching a carrier bag containing some lovely warm Welsh cakes which he proffered to Peter's mum saying they should be eaten with butter and jam or just sugar sprinkled on them. They all gathered around the kitchen table to have a cup of tea and a cake.

"Thank you, Biffy, those were delicious!" Peter's mum said to Biffy whose face went a little red at the compliment.

"Hey, Biffy, I've got something to show you in my room. Is that OK mum? Is the bathroom clean enough for you?"

"You've done a good job Peter, thank you. Alice, what you've done is fine too."

"Thanks mum, Biffy's sister, Rhonda, is coming over so we can help each other with our homework. We'll work in my bedroom as soon as she gets here."

Biffy and Peter took the opportunity to escape and Biffy was amazed when Peter threw back the quilt on his bed and revealed the little dragon who looked up expectantly at them.

"She didn't like it in the rabbit hutch and I can't say I can blame her for that." Peter indicated towards his friend, "This is Biffy." Peter told her, "He helped rescue you from the witch woman and he will be looking after you with me. OK?"

She nodded back at them and then reached across to Biffy's hand and touched it gently with her snout as if making sure she could remember his scent.

"You're rather cute, aren't you? Very tiny though." She seemed to brace herself at that, almost as if she was offended but settled down again when Biffy gave her a little stroke.

"Are you hungry little one?" and out of his pockets he produced some pieces of corned beef saying to Peter, "lucky mum had some of this in the fridge for dad's sandwiches. They won't notice I've taken it." Finnia almost snatched the food out of his hand and swallowed it in a flash. She was a very neat eater, not like Spit who tended to make a rather spluttery mess.

"Was your dad pleased to see you?"

"Hard to tell, but probably not."

Peter had no idea what to say to that. Biffy's relationship with his dad was not a good one.

"Shall we go and make a start on the shed? It's probably safer if we're outside with Finnia when Rhonda is due to come over as we can't take the risk of the girls seeing her and I'm not sure if Finnia's dragon magic will hide her from them." Finnia just looked up at him and he could imagine her thinking, "Just watch me!"

With Finnia hidden inside his jumper the boys clattered down the stairs, calling to Peter's mum that they'd just be outside if she needed them at all.

CHAPTER TEN

They looked first at the rabbit hutch and run, but one glance at Finnia confirmed it wasn't going to be of any use. It was amazing that the tiny dragon managed to express her wishes on that point so very clearly. She hissed at it, swishing her tail backwards and forwards very agitatedly and then turned her back on it. They took her into the small shed and shut themselves in. There wasn't a lot of room for them due to the seemingly huge amount of rubbish surrounding them. Most of it was old toys piled on top of one another and it was difficult to know where to start.

"I suggest that if we pile the things I want to keep on the right side and the ones we can give to the charity shop on the left, that would be a start. Anything that is broken we'll put outside for dad to take to the dump. Best keep it tidy though or mum will be after us!"

Finnia was perched on a shelf where she seemed quite happy and when Peter found a wicker shopping basket he stuffed an old cushion into it and put it on the shelf next to her. She jumped inside and curled up, looking quite contented, her head poking over the top so she could watch them.

"Perhaps she might stay in here when she can't be with us," Peter said to Biffy, "she's obviously not going to go in the rabbit hutch again. Maybe we could sell it."

He glanced up at the little dragon and could have sworn her eyes gleamed brighter at that suggestion.

He started rummaging through the toys and Biffy settled himself down onto an old wooden stool.

Then Biffy's face pulled into a grimace. "We forgot to let Brenda know we got back alright Peter!! She might be worried silly!"

"Oh no! Does that mean we have to sing?" Peter looked out of the door and checked the back of the house. "Phew, there are no windows open so shall we go to the back of the shed and do it now?"

Biffy clambered down from the stool. "Best get it over and done with then!"

Finnia just gazed at them making it obvious she had no intention of moving from such a comfy spot.

They pushed through the brambles next to the rabbit hutch.

"Lucky there's a small wind. Didn't Brenda say we'd need to use a breeze to send our song to her?" Biffy asked.

"Yeah! She did. You start, and I'll join in. Do you want to put your fingers in your ears, so you can't hear me?" Peter was annoyed to see that Biffy did just that before he opened his mouth and sang. As before it sounded rather lovely until Peter joined in when immediately the neighbour's dog started to bark which made Peter giggle and he stopped his toneless tune.

He gave Biffy a nudge. "I don't think our audience liked that!"

"What?" Biffy took his fingers out of his ears and couldn't stop laughing when he heard the dog barking.

"Sensible dog! He doesn't like your singing either! Let's hope that Brenda's magic will hear through the air, despite being so far way. That's one dragon I'd really not want to upset!"

They waited in the silence that surrounded them, not at all sure what to expect and after a moment Peter pointed into the sky.

"Look at that! Just look at that!"

High in the sky were clouds which had formed into a dragon shape, just like Brenda when she was flying. There's our sign!" he announced as they both stared in amazement at the beautifully shaped dragon – was it smiling?! "Amazing and so quick! Dragon magic is certainly something else!"

Feeling rather pleased with themselves they went back to their self-imposed chore and by lunchtime there was quite a reasonable pile of broken toys outside the shed leaving a lot more space inside.

What had amused the boys immensely at one point was that after Peter had gone indoors to make a cup of tea for his parents, he brought one out for himself and Biffy and put the mugs down on the shelf quite near the basket. Finnia had hopped out and reached up over the rim of the closest mug and drunk the contents dry.

"You like tea then little one?" Peter smiled at her and then went back indoors to get another tea for himself, leaving Biffy giggling.

When they were called in for lunch Peter suggested to Finnia that she stayed in the basket, he didn't like to insist.

He thought she looked quite regal and that it wouldn't go down well if he ordered her about like he would a pet. She stared at him with her lovely amythest eyes which were the same as those of the huge dragons, and then nodded her agreement.

"You'll have to get used to being here on your own because after tomorrow I won't be able to take you with me when I go to school. Will that be OK?" She was still for a while until she inclined her head very gracefully again. Peter made very sure he closed the door securely before he went into the house. He couldn't take the risk of a dragon, albeit a very tiny one, following him inside.

There was a lot of laughter over lunch as Rhonda and Alice took the mickey out of Peter and Biffy. They thought it was hilarious that the boys were going to make a den out of the shed and even funnier when they saw the rubbish outside on the ground. Alice suggested that they come along later and have a look at what the boys had done. Peter did his best to try and fob her off by telling her it would be better if they saw the finished article rather than the mess it was in currently but he wasn't at all sure that they were going to take any notice of him.

The lads were soon back inside the shed, and the first thing Peter did was to tell Finnia that if anyone other than Biffy or himself came into the den she had to hide herself away. She needed to keep safe.

The little dragona nodded her understanding.

"It's great that you understand me."

She watched them as they worked stalking backwards and forwards along the shelf and peering down at them every now and them, her tail swishing from side to side.

Both boys were so engrossed in examining one of the old toys that they were totally shocked when the door banged open and their two sisters appeared giggling in the opening.

"Thought you might like some tea and more of Biffy's cakes!"

"That…that's lovely thank you," said Peter politely. He glanced up and saw that thankfully Finnia had hidden herself behind the basket. She must have heard them coming which was more than Biffy and he had done. Biffy too seemed taken aback but was happy to take a Welsh cake laden with butter and jam. It dribbled down his mouth as he ate it and he wiped the mess away with the back of his hand.

The girls stayed for a while to chat to them, or rather torment Peter about the toys he had decided to keep, and he ended up putting his mug on the shelf near the basket while he ate his cake realising that he was not going to get rid of his sister and her friend quickly. When he picked the mug up a little while later and peered into the cup the tea was gone.

"Oh! I must have drunk it all without noticing!" was all he could say. "Don't suppose you fancy making some more do you?"

The answer was a giggle but then Rhonda took the mug from him and went out of the door reappearing shortly afterwards with a full mug of tea.

"Thank you, Rhonda!" He noticed that she blushed at that and looked down quickly at his cup. Although the tea was hot he supposed he'd better drink it straight away or Finnia might get at it again.

CHAPTER ELEVEN

She slept in his bed with him once more that night. When asked if she wanted to stay in the shed, she turned her back on him. She obviously knew her own mind.

The ringing of the church bells woke him early on Sunday and he was out of bed, washed and dressed as quickly as he could.

The tiny dragon watched him, tilting her head at him as she licked her lips.

"Food?" he asked.

She touched her nose to his hand and nodded her reply.

"OK!" he smiled as he picked her up and tucked her inside his jumper.

He raided the fridge where he found some ham and cut a small piece of cheese for her to go with it. It certainly seemed a strange diet for a dragon. He decided to make a pot of tea for his parents and give them a treat by taking it up to them in bed, knocking quietly before entering. They both smiled sleepily at him as they saw the steaming mugs he had in his hands. He'd left Finnia guzzling her very own mug of tea on the kitchen table. It was strange that a dragon would like tea because it most definitely wasn't something that she'd ever have come across before.

For a change of scene, he carried her along the lane to a small culvert that was at the end. It always had water flowing through it. Green spiky reeds covered the bank either side of it and once he found the perfect place to reach right down to the water's edge he placed Finnia there. With no more ado, she scampered into the water to roll about having a whale of a time. If any minnows were foolish enough to swim in a deeper part nearby she would snatch at them, swallowing them whole, much like Peter had seen the much larger dragons of Harris do when they caught a fish in the sea. He smiled when he thought of McDragon's threat to eat seals, he still wasn't sure whether the dragons would really do that or not.

Peter kept guard until she finally clambered out to stand beside his feet. The water streamed from her back and he waited patiently for her to begin to dry in the weak sunlight. She was still quite wet when he picked her up and a damp patch soaked through to his skin but he didn't mind, it was worth it just to see her enjoying herself and catching her own food like wild dragons did.

As he sauntered back towards home he felt that strange tingling in the back of his neck warning him of magic and he shuddered when he saw an odd dark shape crossing the sky in the distance. It was zigzagging as if searching and it was coming closer and closer. Should he run?

Finnia hissed loudly and leapt from his arms to scamper under a nearby bush. As there was no time to get back to the safety of the shed, he threw himself on top of her making sure his body covered every bit of the little dragon to give her as much protection from the magic searcher as possible. He kept very, very still but beneath him he could feel Finnia trembling. When he felt the prickle getting stronger he looked up briefly and felt a moment of panic as the shape materialised into the flying gargoyle.

"The witch's gargoyle." He whispered to her. "How do they know to search for you here?"

No answer of course. It was damp on the ground with early dew and gradually the wet patch on his jumper spread and the smell of mud filled his nostrils. The bramble strands above him began to prickle his head as the squawkin displaced the air around them bouncing the wild blackberry bush.

"Lucky I didn't land on dog poo!" he thought to himself trying not to wriggle.

It was a relief when the tingle dissipated, and he finally allowed himself to relax.

"Do you think it's safe to move now?" he double checked with the little dragon. She was still shivering but managed to nod back at him. Edging carefully out from under the bush Peter stood up and as he brushed himself down he realised he was very damp and a bit smelly. A quick change of clothes was required before his mum saw what a state he was in and asked awkward questions.

In the far distance he could see the squawkin continuing its search, but as he couldn't feel the tingle in his neck he assumed it couldn't sense him either. It would swoop down low every so often and he guessed it was cloaked in magic which hid it from human sight.

"It's lucky we're travelling to Harris next weekend!" he whispered to Finnia. "Hopefully it won't follow us there and the other dragons will be able to help protect you." He stroked her gently as he walked back towards the garden gate still feeling her agitation. It was no wonder she was petrified, the squawkins were very, very scary creatures.

Once at the house he tucked her inside her bed and after stripping off his wet attire and dressing again he nipped down to the kitchen and made her a cup of tea, spooning a couple of teaspoons of sugar into it hoping it would have the same effect as if you gave it to a human who'd had a shock. She sipped it gratefully and gradually relaxed into sleep.

Throughout the day Peter kept an eye out just in case the squawkin returned but there was no sign of it. Finnia, rather surprisingly opted to remain in his room for the whole day and he assumed that she was worn out from her exertions that morning in the water and from the shock of their pursuer being so close. Biffy, when he arrived, was dismayed to hear of their narrow escape and the boys took it in turn to nip up to Peter's room to check on the little thing as they continued their work in the shed, chatting nonstop the whole time.

"She certainly seemed scared when she saw the squawkin," Peter told his friend. "It makes me wonder why the witch has been hunting for her."

That night Peter contacted Seraphina to see if she had any advice for him but, unfortunately there was none other than the sooner he took Finnia to the Outer Hebrides, the better. McDragon or Effel may have more of an idea but so far there had been no sign of either of them.

CHAPTER TWELVE

The days until they went away seemed to drag on until at last, they were off to the Isle of Harris. Peter's mum and Alice had opted to stay at home because Alice needed to study for some tests at school and as the trip was only for just over a week it was better that she studied at home. Rhonda would be there too. The good side of their being only the three of them was that Biffy could have the whole of the back seat to himself, leaving Peter in the front next to his dad.

It felt so nice to be away from the worry of the gargoyle hunting for Finnia so near the house. It hadn't reappeared since that first sighting, but Peter was constantly concerned that it would return.

It was a relief to them all when they eventually turned off of the boring motorway and began the next part of their journey heading towards the ferry.

The most amusing part of the trip for Peter was that every so often a not very nice smell filled the car and Peter's dad would immediately open his window and then stare through the rear view mirror at Biffy. Biffy took no notice the first time but when the smell surrounded them again he said, "Pardon me!" and opened his window too. Peter twisted in his seat to look at Biffy who shrugged his shoulders as if to say, "Wasn't me!" and nodded his head back to the rear of the car. It kept happening, and repeatedly Peter had to struggle to swallow a giggle because they'd obviously made a bit of a mistake feeding Finnia some fishy cat food the day before. When they'd offered it to her, she'd sniffed at it for quite a while before deciding to go ahead and eat it. Obviously, she'd been right in her hesitation seeing as it had had a very unfortunate effect on her tummy. They hadn't needed to ask the Scottish dragons to use their magic to put her to sleep because she had agreed without any fuss at all that she would be quiet and keep hidden in the back of the car.

Having eaten on the ferry as usual and then having a brief shop for extra groceries in Tarbert, the three of them eventually traipsed along the footpath carrying their luggage. Finnia was hidden on the top of Peter's bag. It wasn't long before Biffy was puffing away like a steam engine but he did manage to keep up. Thankfully, Peter's dad opted to do the second trip back to the car on his own as he felt the need to stretch his legs some more after that long drive.

Outside the cottage Finnia was released so that she too could move about and do whatever business she needed to. The boys left her scampering about getting her bearings while they put the kettle on and got plates and cups out for a restorative cup of tea.

The tea was left brewing as they went upstairs to unpack. Biffy was going to use the room which Alice considered as hers for their short stay on the island.

Peter peered out of his bedroom window as he unpacked, looking down at McDragon's rocks but it was hard to tell if the dragon was there or not – he was desperate to take Finnia down to introduce her to his great dragon friend.

Before Peter's dad returned Peter snuck a mug of tea out to Finnia now that it seemed to be her favourite drink. She would miss that when she lived with the other dragons, Peter thought to himself.

Once his dad sank thankfully into an armchair and put his feet up on a pouffe he told the boys that he was going to have a short nap and they could go down to the beach, but they had to promise not to go any further than that.

They were very happy to be outside and although they both needed jackets there was a gentle breeze and no rain. Finnia curled herself around Peter's neck so that she could see everything. Sheep called to one another as they passed them, some of them scampering away. They looked very fat and ready to burst so maybe they were close to producing lambs. The peep peep of the oyster catchers as they flew swiftly across the top of the sea to land on rocks the other side of the beach was a very familiar sound. No gannets to be seen though and Peter told Biffy that it was probably a bit early for them, maybe they wanted to arrive at the same time as when the mackerel came into the bay. In the distance there was cawing but not how crows normally sounded when they chattered together. Peter swung his binoculars up to see what could be causing it. As they came into view, he felt sure that the big black birds hopping about on the craggy top of the hill looked like ravens. He'd not seen them before.

They continued down to the little beach. The tide was out which meant the black and yellow rocks were completely on show, dark lines of seaweed hanging from them.

McDragon's rocks loomed to one side and just as the boys reached them, the rocks began to melt away until the magnificent dragon stood before them.

Peter began the dragon hum and Biffy joined in. Then to Peter's amazement he felt a vibration through Finnia and her hum reverberated around them. McDragon sang his welcome too. It was a lovely warming sound.

"Good morning, Petersmith and Master Biffy! And, welcome to you too, McFinnia!" A very surprised look crossed Peter's face – Finnia must be a Scottish dragon to be called McFinnia.

Finnia nodded her head and hopped down from Peter's shoulders to stand before McDragon. She was minute by comparison. The big dragon dropped his head down allowing her to clamber up starting at his snout until she delicately made her way to where his neck met his huge body.

"I am glad you have finally arrived, Petersmith. I have been away on dragon business but I flew back via Seraphina's island and she told me your news. It is very fortunate you have brought McFinnia here to stay with us so that we can give her the protection she needs."

Rather surprisingly there was a loud hiss from Finnia from her perch on top of the big dragon and McDragon bent his neck round to peer at her looking quite surprised at her response.

"Petersmith, I think you and Master Biffy should leave us so that McFinnia and I can converse. I believe we have much to talk about as she obviously has some ideas of her own. If you visit me tomorrow morning Petersmith, I will fly you to see your good friend, Spit. He is very keen to see you, as I am sure you are him."

"Thank you, McDragon. You are right, I would love to do that." He looked at Finnia briefly and added, "Is that OK with you, Finnia?"

The tiny dragon nodded her head regally in reply.

"Master Biffy?"

"Yes, McDragon?

"I regret I cannot take you to the island too as I can only manage to fly one lad that far."

"No matter, McDragon, I can stay in bed for longer, but thank you for thinking of me."

There was nothing for it after that but for the boys to head back to the cottage. Peter felt rather lost without the little dragon, but he guessed he was going to have to get used to that feeling if she was remaining on the Isle of Harris.

"Well, that was short and sweet, wasn't it?" Biffy muttered.

Peter grunted back at him.

"It's OK, Dragon boy, you'll get to see her again tomorrow. I think I'll make a cake – your dad will like that."

CHAPTER THIRTEEN

Their flight the next morning was as exhilarating as it usually was. Peter flung both arms out either side of him, sitting up nice and straight and loving the feeling of the air rushing through his hair and almost pushing him backwards. He was nicely warm because McDragon had huffed heat over him before he'd done his ungainly scramble up onto the dragon's back, hampered slightly as usual by his dodgy hand. But once on top, the dragon scales by his knees clenched down to grip him firmly in place. Finnia was already on board but she sidled over to Peter and pushed herself into his jacket keeping her head peeking over the top. The wind during their flight would have swept her away if she'd not done that.

Peter shouted with joy!

"You enjoy flying then Petersmith?" McDragon's voice boomed in his head.

"Oh, most definitely, McDragon! Flying with you is the best!"

As he closed his mouth out of the corner of his eye he saw something hurtling towards them.

"Enemy to the right!"

"I see it. Hold on tight, I will have to engage it in battle."

Peter grabbed hold of the spiny upright scale on McDragon's neck and bent down low.

"Stay hidden, Finnia. We are under attack." he spoke quietly to her.

Their attacker was a large squawkin, its lethal talons pointing towards them as McDragon dove to the left to avoid it. As he did his long tail swept out and lashed at the squawkin shoving it off course and its horrible scream followed them as it began to spiral downwards.

McDragon kept close behind it, ready to whack it again if it looked like it was going to recover and come back after them. When it had almost crashed into the sea the squawkin pulled itself up and then shot off back the way it had come.

"Phew! That was close, McDragon! You batted that out of the way very well, perhaps you should take up cricket!"

He felt the big dragon vibrate as if he was laughing and once he had them flying towards their destination again he said into Peter's head, "They have taken to coming after us more often recently, but fortunately only single squawkins at any time. It will become a problem if there is more than one."

"Why are they attacking more frequently? Do you have any idea?"

"No, but I guess that evil wizard, McMuran, is behind it, as before."

Finnia's head peaked out of Peter's jacket and Peter told her that the danger was over for the time being. He explained that the squawkin that had chased after them was much larger than the ones which had been hunting for her when she was with Brenda.

On the horizon Peter spotted the familiar sight of Seraphina's hideaway and he began to get quite excited, pointing it out to Finnia.

McDragon began his dive down to land very neatly on the island.

"Your landings are very good now, McDragon," Peter praised him, "much better than they used to be."

He received just a hurummph in response.

As soon as McDragon came to a halt Peter could hear dragon talons rasping along the ground going at quite a pace and a very exuberant Spit lolloped into view. He stopped in front of the black dragon and bent his head to begin the dragon greeting and Peter joined in, as did Finnia. Spit kept staring at her, quite fascinated to see such a small being but then the hum grew louder as Seraphina, Haribald d'Ness and Popple came into the small clearing.

As soon as the song was over, Peter felt the scales over his knees release him and he slid to the ground.

"How do you do, Spit?" he called.

"Very well, thank you Petersmith!" and he lifted one of his front feet out to Peter who clenched his knuckles and bumped his hand against a talon. That started Spit off doing his dragon giggle and his tail started to swish from side to side beginning to raise a dust storm.

As Peter spluttered Spit had the sense to still his tail.

"Good day, Seraphina and Haribald!" Peter called to them at the same time bending down to give Popple, who had sidled over to him, a kiss on the top of her head. She'd grown but she was still very small in dragon terms. He felt

Finnia wriggle inside his jacket as if to ask to be released and he unzipped it and placed her on the ground. She was much smaller than Popple, but she bowed her head regally to the adult dragons and they in turn bowed back.

Without even turning her head to look at Peter, Finnia immediately followed the large dragons back to the overhang where they usually held their pow wows. McDragon went after them, instructing Peter and Spit to play nicely together. Popple sensibly moved out of range as Spit promptly barrelled into Peter rolling about on the ground. It was a game he particularly enjoyed although Peter wasn't so sure it was one he liked so much now that Spit had grown in size.

"Spit, stop for a minute! How about giving me a flying demonstration?"

"Good thinking, Petersmith!" Spit replied proudly, about to leap off the ground just as a loud "Caw" came from the direction of the rocks down by the sea. Archie flew into view and promptly settled lightly on Peter's shoulder.

"Hello, Archie! How are you?" Archie nudged Peter gently with his beak. He was a black crow which a white streak down his wing – the white streak made him a target as far as other crows were concerned, and he used to be bullied by them, much as Spit had been when he lived in McMuran's magic bubble and as Peter had been at school. Archie was nearly always found wherever the young dragon was.

CHAPTER FOURTEEN

As always, McDragon returned Peter to the Isle of Harris so that he could "break his fast" as McDragon called it. Dragon time was amazing – Peter's dad had no idea at all that Peter had been gone so long but Peter was always ravenous when he got back from his travels with the dragons. He walked in just in time for his breakfast to be served up. Biffy raised his eyebrows as if in a question as Peter sat down beside him smiling and nodding his reply.

The phone rang as they finished their breakfast, so Peter's dad left the room leaving the boys obligingly clearing the table and washing up. They chatted quietly as they did their chores, Peter explaining that Finnia had remained on the island with Seraphina, Haribald and their two young charges. Peter felt rather sad because the tiny dragon had ignored him completely after their arrival and hadn't responded when Peter had made his goodbyes once McDragon had deemed it time to leave.

Their chat was interrupted by the return of Peter's dad.

"I think you'll like this, boys! That was Alistair and he says that a friend of his who is staying with him is going to visit one of the small islands further out today and Alistair suggested that he takes you with him. Rory will enjoy having the company and that means you can do something fun while I get on with my work today. Assuming you're both happy with that plan, let's set too and get some lunch prepared for you to take with you. We'll meet Alistair at Tarbert harbour and he'll introduce you to Rory. Apparently, Rory is a mine of information as far as the islands and wildlife are concerned."

They were soon in the car speeding down towards the harbour where Alistair was waiting patiently for them.

Rory had a weather beaten but kind looking face which was topped by carrot red hair. He beamed when he was introduced to the boys, telling them that he was actually Murdo McMuran's cousin. That sent a warning shiver up and down Peter's spine, but there was nothing he could do but politely shake the man's hand. There was no feeling of magic as he did, not like when he'd touched McMuran's, so maybe this redhaired man was as nice as he seemed.

"So, where is Murdo at the moment?" Peter's dad enquired. "I tried to ring him to let him know that we were here and to thank him for his help before but there was no answer."

"Oh, he's in Wales currently. Another distant cousin was in touch with him as it seems she has a problem she needs help with, so he's gone to see what he can do. They'll have a lot to talk about because they have similar interests."

Peter exchanged a glance with Biffy. Was it just co-incidence that the witch woman lived in Wales? She obviously had an interest in dragons.

"I'll have the boys back with you in time for their tea," Rory added.

The lads were soon buckled into life jackets and strapped into seats alongside Rory. They were in a black RIB, (a rigid inflatable boat) which seemed to fly across the sea, spray splattering into their faces. Peter put his worries aside and tipped his head back to open his mouth – it felt wonderful – nearly as good as riding a dragon but not quite. Biffy on the other hand looked rather green and held on to the edges of his seat with knuckles that were white from where he gripped so hard. His body was rigid, whereas Peter just let himself go with the flow. He thought it was a fabulous way to travel.

"Glad you could come along!" Rory shouted across to the lads, glancing briefly at Biffy's rigid frame. "Don't worry Biffy, this is quite a safe way to travel and very fast too, just try and relax into the movement of the RIB but if you do think you're going to be sick please can you get it over the side rather than inside?" Biffy nodded, not really reassured as he seemed to grip the seat even tighter.

As they skimmed the sea Peter studied their new friend. A smile crossed his face as he imagined Spit rolling about in amusement if he'd seen them shaking hands and saying the words "How do you do!" when they were introduced.

"Do you enjoy being here in the Outer Hebrides?" Rory asked.

"Definitely, we love it here," answered Peter.

"Don't you think it's dragon country?"

Peter kept his face as neutral as he could at that comment and made sure he didn't look over at Biffy. It seemed like a very strange thing for an adult to say and more alarm bells rang in his head.

"That's the sort of thing Peter would say," Biffy answered without giving his reply any thought, obviously trying to take his mind away from the bouncing across the waves.

"Really!" was Rory's response as he looked enquiringly at Peter. "When I was a young lad I used to spend a lot of time looking for dragons," and he winked at Biffy before he looked across at Peter. "Have you found any yet?"

Biffy snorted as he tried to deflect the gaze of the big man to himself.

"Dragons! Nuts all of you!" he announced grinning broadly. "What about you, did you ever find any?" he responded and then, "Where would you suggest we look?"

A guffaw of laughter was an answer, "I kept looking and looking, I still do sometimes, even now, but I've not come across any as yet, but I'm sure they're out there somewhere! Let me know if you see one, won't you?"

It wasn't long before they slowed to pass the tall rocky stacks where the gannets and other seabirds nested in their thousands, swooping down into the grey that was lapping at the base of the white guano topped rocks. They were incredibly noisy, but fascinating to watch. Peter looked up trying to see if these were the same stacks which Effel had had to rest on when she was flying with him last time they were there. He didn't think they were but they looked much the same.

Picking up speed they were off again, and Peter was shocked to realise they were heading to a very familiar island – McMuran's island was on the horizon!

As they slowed to approach the island Peter tried not to let the sheer panic that he was feeling show on his face – his last memories of being here were not good ones! What's more they seemed to be aiming towards the side of the island where the cavern was rather than to the harbour. Was Rory in league with McMuran and trying to capture them?

The small boat slowly chugged into the beautiful cave with the amazing coloured stalactites spearing down from the roof due to all the minerals that had dripped into the sea over hundreds of years. Their last view of the cave had been on the day that Biffy had helped with the rescue of Popple, McDragon and Peter from the wizard, McMuran's clutches.

Peter and Biffy looked around them – there was not a gargoyle in sight, which raised the question, where were the squawkins?

"Amazingly beautiful, isn't it?" Rory smiled at the boys.

"It is," agreed Peter, forcing himself to look relaxed. "The last time we were here was when the captain from our last trip brought us." He hoped his nose wouldn't grow with the lie or he'd look like the witch.

"After that we saw the dolphins," Biffy chimed in.

"It's always a treat when they appear. I still love it when they're around even though I've seen them many, many, times over the years!"

Rory leapt out of the boat onto the small dock and tied the boat up neatly and speedily. Then he held out his hand indicating to the boys that they could now disembark.

It felt good to be on dry land, but Peter was very much on guard against what was going to happen next.

Their host pointed towards the rear of the small landing area and the two friends hung back a little as if they had never been there before, but Rory flicked his fingers as if to say, "Go on!"

There was no option but to move onwards very slowly being aware that they were heading towards the tunnel which lead to the cavern where Peter and Popple had been imprisoned.

"Not that way boys!" Rory had caught up with them and tugged at Peter's shoulder, "That way's a real maze and you could get lost in the tunnels that seem to go on forever. Even I've never been down them all," and turned Peter to the far left and almost back on himself. There in front of them were some narrow stone steps which Peter hadn't seen before as they were quite hidden in the shadows.

"Phew!" Peter thought to himself, feeling the tension drain out of him as if a plug had been pulled.

The steps led to a small wooden door which creaked open displaying a very dark corridor in front of them. It was so very black they couldn't see much further than a few feet ahead but then Rory took a step forward and lights sprang up either side of the stone walls.

"Come on then boys! Put your best foot forward!"

"How do those lights work?" Biffy enquired of their host.

"Magic, I guess! Maybe dragon magic!" Rory chortled. "Actually, I have no idea! I do have a torch with me just in case, but they've always been activated automatically like that every time I've been here – and that's been some years, as many a time I came with Murdo when we were boys. I have a standing invitation to visit whenever I want to, which I do as often as I can."

The floor of the tunnel was quite flat and smooth, as were the walls and the tunnel seemed to go on forever. To pass the time Rory chatted about this and that as they marched forward, and when they were quiet between conversations the sound of Biffy's panting echoed around them.

"Are we under the sea?" Peter queried.

"I believe so. You'll be very surprised when we arrive at our destination, and I can promise you it's well worth waiting for!"

"I certainly hope so," Biffy groaned.

Peter got the sense that they were now on an incline and that became more obvious as Biffy's breath began to get more and more ragged.

"Nearly at the end of this bit, laddies!" Rory said encouragingly.

A short while later another wooden door confronted them. Biffy took the opportunity to bend right over, hands on his thighs trying to get his breath.

Rory lifted the wooden latch and the door creaked open revealing stone steps spiralling upwards. When Peter looked above them he could see daylight in the centre of the twirling steps and he had to hide his smile as he imagined how Biffy was going to feel once he realised he had to climb up and up.

"Who built these steps, they look very old!"

"They are hundreds of years old and I, for one, have no idea whose brainchild they were. Of course, it's not so easy to see the way up when it's a dark or cloudy day and what's more, the staircase can be pretty lethal if it's raining. We'll take it slowly so that Biffy can keep up."

As the puffing sound started up again, Rory stopped and said kindly, "Biffy, let me take your backpack – I rather think it might be a bit too much for you to carry up these stairs." Biffy gratefully passed over the bag, and Rory laughed as he took it, "What have you got in here laddie? Rocks?"

"It's cake, which I made myself!" Biffy announced proudly.

Rory must have realised he had touched a nerve and just said, "Well, I shall look forward to trying that." And with that they began their ascent.

The steam train that was behind them showed what an enormous effort it was for poor Biffy, and there was a great deal of groaning which meant that they had to stop to rest every so often to give him a chance to try and catch his breath. Peter was very happy to find he wasn't doing too badly himself. Privately he thought that it wouldn't do Biffy any harm to do more walking and he believed that his mate needed to balance out his love of food and cooking with a little more exercise, although he couldn't tell him that without offending him.

It was a relief to everyone when they finally reached the fresh air at the very top and Biffy threw himself onto a nearby grassy verge to prostrate himself as he tried to recover his breath.

"Well, what do you think then lads? Was it worth the hike?"

CHAPTER FIFTEEN

The vista surrounding them was jaw dropping and Peter's backpack slipped from his shoulders and fell on the floor as he stared about them.

"Wow!"

To his complete amazement they were on another island which overlooked what must be McMuran's island with only a small expanse of rough sea between them. It looked almost as if with a good leap one could jump from one island to the other, though he certainly wasn't going to try that – it would be a long fall down into a very, very cold sea.

Behind him, standing clearly against the skyline were the remains of a castle and… were they…? Peter stared some more and… yes, aligned along the battlements around the one remaining turret were about half a dozen stone dragons facing out to sea as if they were keeping an eye on the other island. The other walls adjoining the turret were in different states of disrepair, some seemed to be holding up better than others, and scattered across the ground in front of the castle were large lumps of white stone which must have toppled down as the walls collapsed over the years.

"Definitely, a big wow! Biffy you need to get off the ground and have a look – this old castle is absolutely amazing!!"

"Thought you'd like it," Rory announced proudly. "I've been coming here since I was a wee laddie and it never ceases to amaze me that nothing changes. As far as I am aware, there are the same number of broken slabs littering the ground as there were all those years ago. I counted them once to try and check it out, but I've forgotten the numbers now."

"So, did we walk all the way under the sea from over there," Peter pointed at the other island, "to get here?"

"Aye!"

"This island seems to be the identical twin of that one – how fascinating. But it wasn't visible from the sea, was it?"

"No, it's always shrouded in mist and seems to merge into the sea and sky somehow. Murdo and I have tried so many different approaches, but it never comes into view at all. See, more magic I guess!"

"Gosh! Who on earth could have tunnelled all the way across here?"

"I've no idea but it's very clever isn't it? It meant that the people who built this castle, along with what appears to be a replica of the one over there," and he pointed behind the house on the other island, "didn't need to rely on a boat to get from one island to the other."

"Wow, maybe you're right, it is magic!"

Rory gave a small smile, "That's just what I always thought, although Murdo always pooh poohed that idea."

"How old do you think it is?"

"I canna say, it's very, very ancient."

A very satisfied sigh puffed from the young man just as Biffy finally lifted his head briefly from the ground and grunted his approval.

"Can I explore?" Peter asked his host itching to be away.

"Go ahead but be careful of all the fallen slabs of rock, I don't fancy carrying you back down those steps and through the passageway under the sea. I've never yet found another way to get on or off this island." He stared away into the distance as he added, "Now laddies, I think you're old enough for me to leave you for a short while so as I can check out the bird life, which is really why I came today. There are a large number of seabirds which nest in the rocks on the cliff the other side of the island and I want to make sure they're not on the decline. It's an interest of mine. I won't be too long but try shouting very loudly if you need me and I'll hopefully hear you and come running."

"That's fine Rory," the boys chorused as Rory strode off along a narrow path that went in the opposite direction from where they'd come from.

"You should take a proper look, Biffy – I'm going exploring!"

"I will, but first I'm going to have a short nap," a rather red-faced Biffy muttered, obviously still rather short of breath, "I'm going to need to recover so I can manage the return journey, I think." Peter snorted as if agreeing and then pointed out a mossy bank just behind some rocks a short way off which might be more comfortable for Biffy and then he headed off towards the fascinating castle's turret.

The steps wending their way up to it were worn in the middle, as if from years and years of feet going up and down them and he had this strange sensation niggling at him, almost drawing him up them and giving him the feeling of urgency at the same time.

At the top he fumbled about in his pocket and dragged out his trusty binoculars to stare across at McMuran's island. From this angle what had been hidden previously were the remnants of the castle Rory had told him about. It wasn't in such good a condition as this one, but, wait, were those shapes he could spy near the top stone gargoyles? He adjusted the sighting of his binoculars. Yes, he was right, and they were facing this way! He shuddered at the thought of them coming alive.

"This is what it must have looked like thousands of years ago," he muttered to himself. "I can't wait to tell McDragon about it!"

He reached down absentmindedly to stroke the head of one of the stone dragons beside him, much as he would have done if it had been Popple next to him.

Just beyond where the dragons were lined up was an arched opening and he moved carefully along to it. Thrusting his head through the gap he gasped with delight – there was a circular room inside and spread across the whole of the floor was a huge star. What's more, bang in the centre of the star with the light from the window illuminating it stood a stone lectern. It had a flat top, perfect for a big book to sit there as if waiting to be read. It was too tempting – he just had to get in.

Peter squeezed himself through the narrow gap – it was a very tight fit and he grazed his hand on the window ledge as he squashed himself through to the other side, wiping the blood from the cut which was oozing out, onto his trousers.

His dragon kin senses seemed to have come alive as soon as he had stepped into the room.

The room was in semi darkness but as he tilted his head to stare up at the ceiling above him he whispered to himself, "A dragon!" There spread right above him was the etching of what could almost have been McDragon himself. As he stared it seemed to glow and illuminate the room with a gentle light. His neck tingled as he examined it and his imagination began to run riot. He could picture a wizard with a pointy hat and long robe covered with stars standing at the lectern, reading a big tome, his wand resting next to the book.

"Oh gosh!" Just the thought of being here inside something which had been built so long ago sent shivers up his spine.

He looked down through the window and some way away he spotted Biffy's foot poking out from behind a huge boulder. He must have taken Peter's advice and settled himself down there taking both the backpacks with him because they were nowhere in sight.

Peter had no idea how long he'd been inside the turret room absorbing everything around him when a noise distracted him – it came from the direction of where they'd emerged from the tunnel.

"No!!"

With a huge intake of breath his heart began to pound loudly as panic flooded through his body.

"McMuran!" he breathed quietly, and then, "That cannot be!" because beside him strode the red cloaked witch woman swinging her stick in time with her marching footsteps, much as she had when they saw her in Wales!!! McMuran's kilt was swaying gaily from side to side as he headed towards the ruins of the castle.

What should he do? There was no way he could get out of the window without being seen and it was terrifying to imagine what would happen to him if the wizard caught him here. He looked down at Biffy's foot which hadn't moved at all. He could only hope his friend remained asleep and that Rory stayed away studying the birdlife on the cliffs.

The witch and wizard were nearly at the foot of the castle steps! He needed to think – and fast!

There was a sort of alcove which must have been used for a fire in olden times as the back was a very sooty colour – it was to one side of the window opening. He moved over and pressed himself tightly against the wall. Then he put his hand into his pocket until it connected with the large dragon scale which was there.

His heart was pumping nineteen to the dozen and he shuddered as he heard footsteps beginning to ascend the outer steps.

Pushing his back more firmly against the cold stone wall, he just hoped Seraphina could help him or he was in big, big trouble.

CHAPTER SIXTEEN

He was in luck, Seraphina answered him immediately.

"Petersmith, do you have need of me?"

"Seraphina, it's an emergency! Please can you hide me from sight using dragon magic? And quickly! McMuran is approaching and is nearly upon me and he has the witch woman with him!"

The dragoness was silent momentarily as she took in the desperation in his voice. Then, "Petersmith, I will do my best but do not move from where you are, and while I am doing this you must repeat to yourself again and again, 'I am invisible! I am invisible!' Start now Petersmith, and do not stop until they are gone! We can only hope my magic is strong enough to reach you. Be warned though, you may feel rather faint once my magic is taken away, as is likely to happen to me too."

Peter stood as still as a statue trying to breathe very quietly as he began the mantra in his head over, and over again. "I am invisible! I am invisible! I am invisible!"

He squeezed his eyes shut for a moment and when he opened them again his view of the room was rather blurry. Was this because the dragon magic was working?

He concentrated on repeating the words in his head, "I am invisible! I am invisible!" all the time trying not to panic. His eyesight became sharper and everything was incredibly clear.

The footsteps seemed so much louder than before – had the dragon magic altered his hearing too? He could smell soot too – so maybe his sense of smell had changed as well.

Fortunately, he knew the window opening was far too small for an adult to climb through, but he had no idea if there was another way into this turret room. He certainly hadn't seen one when he'd been examining the room.

"Well, this was certainly worth waiting for. I had no idea this island was here, behind your one!" the witch woman's lilting Welsh brogue wafted over to Peter. He could hear her speaking clearly despite the thick stone wall that was between them. He flinched as he glimpsed the top of her head appearing through the window twisting backwards and forwards as she surveyed the room.

As she took her time scanning the room, Peter tried to breathe as lightly as possible while making a huge effort not to move any part of his body, repeating his mantra in his head as he did whilst keeping a tight clasp on the dragon scale in his hand. Whatever happened he must not let go of it!

"I am invisible! I am invisible! I am invisible!"

"Is there any way we can get inside, Murdo?" she asked.

"The last time I got in was when I was a wee boy and could fit through that gap. I've never discovered how the wizard who built the castle entered the room. I've searched and searched but I canna find a door." Peter would have recognised McMuran's voice anywhere – he frequently had nightmares about it.

He stumbled over the words of his mantra at the mention of a wizard, but then pulled himself together and continued– he knew he mustn't hesitate under any circumstances – he was in an incredibly dangerous situation.

"That's a shame. Perhaps I could summon one of my pets and we can return when it arrives. I can magic them small enough to get through the gap – their eyesight is so much keener than ours so maybe they would spot something you missed as a lad. What a pity you cannot alter the size of your beasts in the same way."

McMuran murmured what sounded like his agreement adding that, anyway, he felt that there would be no benefit in her calling her squawkins away from their tasks. He had searched thoroughly inside when he was a boy and, in more recent years, the walls outside. Peter felt that his tone seemed to convey some reluctance in returning with her.

"Oh look, there's fresh blood on this stone." Peter froze as he glimpsed her head pulling back and then heard her sniff loudly. Was she sniffing at his blood with that droopy nose of hers? How gross!

"It must have been an injured bird that brushed against it. As you saw, the island is not visible to any boats which come close nor is there any way that I have ever found to get here other than through the passageway, so I cannot imagine any human being able to come up here."

"It doesn't smell like animal blood, but… maybe you could be right." She sounded very doubtful.

"Are these stone dragons out here anything like the one that you're searching for? They're what I really brought you to look at."

The witch answered, "No, these are bigger than the special one. I think it will be smaller and much more delicate looking, at least that's what I gleaned from my pets. It's taken me years of research to track it down and then it just vanished with no trace! My squawkins kept trailing the dragon that lives in the mountains near to my home, but so far, they haven't located her hideaway. She's at the bottom of its disappearance, I'm sure!"

"The fact that there are stone dragons here and then the gargoyles on your old castle gives me the feeling that this is exactly the place to help with my research into the little dragons. I really do feel that if we can return and spend some time here together we may come up with something to aid us both."

"Well, I did explain when you twisted my arm to come here that there would be hardly any time at all to look around today but at least you've now seen all there is to see. When we were young Rory used to be with me and we'd spend hours hunting for another way to get into the room. Of course," and McMuran sounded amused, "he never realised what this place really was."

"Well, he wouldn't, would he? He has no magic."

"Probably just as well, he wouldn't approve of some of my methods – he can be a bit of a wimp sometimes! He rang me to say he's visiting some friends in Tarbert currently and as he knows I so very rarely go there, he'll be in touch if he wants us to meet up."

Peter found this insight fascinating – so it was as he had thought – there was no magic in Rory, he was what he was and nothing more, which was a very good thing from their point of view, he just hoped that Rory didn't mention the fact that he'd brought the boys to the island because that could cause a very big problem.

"Apart from these stone dragons have you ever seen any other sign of dragons on this island, maybe an etching or something?"

"No, the closest thing has been the dragon skeleton on my island that I told you about, I can take you there on our way back. Anyhow, I've no proof apart from a mention in my predecessor's old notes that he believed the dragon whose bones they are could have come from here. The bones have been in their resting place a long, long time. The diary also suggests that that dragon had been lured across to my island by some intricate spell but I'm still investigating that."

"When you find out would you be able to share the information with me please? That could come in very useful! Very useful indeed!"

"Of course, although its been taking me a long time to trawl through those old diaries and notes and so far, I haven't found anything of use, but I'll keep looking. Anyhow, one of the theories which was handed down to me when I was a boy was that in days of old, the gargoyles on my castle fought with the dragons on this one. I told Rory about it years ago and we would play a game of dragons and gargoyles – he'd be on the side of the dragons and I'd have the gargoyles at my command, of course."

Peter stared up at the ceiling – couldn't they see the huge dragon etched into the stone there? How come it was only visible to him?

"Where did you find that dragon egg that you told me the boy stole from you? Was it from here?"

"Ah… that's a story for another day, I think! We'd best be away soonish or else there won't be time for me to show you the dragon bones. I've never shown them to Rory or taken him inside the magical dome where they rest."

"Can you give me just a moment… I'm sure I can sense something in here – something familiar." Her head reappeared through the window.

Peter froze and stumbled with the words of his mantra, could she be aware of him somehow? Was it because he was deemed as dragon kin? He restarted the words again very quickly as he watched the top of her head turning this way and that, stilling every so often to allow her eagle eyes to focus on the room. It must have given her a real crick in the neck when she decided to gaze at the ceiling. She was there so long he was able to study her – the long red plait that tied her hair back from her face swung so low it swept from side to side on the floor.

Peter was becoming quite agitated – he was so worried that Rory might return or that Biffy would wake.

At long last her head disappeared.

"There is definitely something here which is tickling at me, but I've no idea what it can be. The ceiling draws my gaze but there is only smooth plain stone to see."

She grunted and then muttered, "Thank you Murdo – how fascinating this all is! Shame the dragons aren't really what I'm looking for, but this room is very interesting… very interesting indeed! There is a lot of history here and my gut tells me it must have something to do with the dragons which interest the both of us so much. I'm never wrong when it comes to dragons!"

Their voices gradually became a murmur as the footsteps faded so Peter guessed that the unwelcome visitors were finally leaving.

The witch continued to badger McMuran for more information about the dragon egg, but he wouldn't relent, and seemed loathe to tell her anything. He obviously wanted to keep that story close to his chest. Shame in a way because Peter would have loved to know how and where McMuran had come across Popple's Pearl.

Uttering a sigh of relief, he allowed himself to wriggle about as he tried to get movement back into his legs. He stopped his mantra and gradually as the dragon magic left him, his vision returned to normal he wobbled out of his hidey-hole and slunk down onto his haunches dropping his head into his hands.

"Thank you, Seraphina, they are gone!" he muttered and rather thought he heard her give a sigh of relief too.

As soon as he felt more himself, he struggled to his feet and peeked around the edge of the arched window and was just in time to catch a glimpse of the wizard and witch disappearing down the steps leading to the tunnel. His hearing must have returned to normal because he no longer had any idea what they were saying to one another.

"Are you alright, Petersmith?" Seraphina's soft voice came over to him.

"Yes, thank you very much Seraphina. Your magic was amazing and hid me well. It took the stuffing out of me when I stopped the mantra, but my head is beginning to clear now."

"I thought that would be the case. I, too, was affected by sending that much magic to you. Normally it would take two dragons to do that. Now I must rest."

Peter relaxed his tight hold on the dragon scale and very slowly and carefully began to walk about the circular room, using the walls to keep him upright. As his fingers caressed the smooth surface much to his delight dragon pictures started to materialise under his hands. The dragons were all different sizes and colours – some were sitting on their hindquarters, some were flying, some had fish in their mouths and there were those that had flames emitting from their snouts. Amongst them one dragon particularly caught his gaze – it was much smaller than the other dragons and had a more delicate shape. "Finnia!" he whispered to himself. Even the colour was the same.

He stared at the image for a long while drinking in the beauty of her before he wandered into the centre of the room where the lectern stood. It felt quite tactile to his touch which was a surprise seeing as it was made of stone and he enjoyed the feeling of his hand smoothing over the top of the flat surface, imagining the wizard who might have stood in the exact place doing the same. Rather strangely he felt that tingle which indicated there was some magic near him. He stared down at the pure white stone top trying to see what it was that was pulling at his senses. In the righthand corner was a mark and when he brought his head closer to it he saw it was the etching of a tiny dragon. Peter touched it gently with his thumb and nearly fell over in fright as the floor beneath him trembled and some of the slabs began to slide smoothly away!

Clinging tightly onto the lectern top he realised he was being turned slowly in a clockwise direction and the stone he was standing on was gradually taking him downwards.

Round and round it turned until the movement ceased and the slab came to a gentle halt.

Two passageways lead away on either side of him illuminated by similar lights that had been in the tunnel between the islands.

A voice echoed high above him, "Hiya, Dragon boy, whatcha doing? Thought you'd want to know that Rory is on his way back – I can hear him singing to himself."

CHAPTER SEVENTEEN

The boys were exhausted and very windswept by the time they returned to the cottage.

There had been groans of disappointment when they'd eventually had to tramp back down the tunnel – Peter being on tenderhooks the whole way back, but luck was with them and there'd been no sign of McMuran or the witch. Rory had handed them back into Peter's dad's care at the harbour in Tarbert, having been thanked very enthusiastically by the boys for taking them to such a super place. Before he walked off he had mentioned quietly to Peter's dad and the boys that he'd decided not to mention their little adventure to his cousin if he did happen to bump into him. Although he had an open invitation to visit the island sometimes Murdo could be quite touchy about it. Both Peter and Biffy smiled and agreed that if they saw him they wouldn't say anything either – they were both very definite on that!

Walking from the car to the cottage the boys trailed behind Peter's dad hoping they'd be able to talk quietly together. Up until now they'd had no time on their own so Peter had only been able to whisper to a very shocked Biffy that McMuran had brought the witch to look at the castle – no other details.

Peter had just begun his tale when his dad stopped walking and waited for them to catch him up.

"You two never stop talking, do you?" he grinned at them. "So how did you enjoy riding in the RIB?"

"It was a bit bouncy for me!" Biffy answered.

That made Peter laugh as he answered, "You were looking a little green, Biffy!"

"That's an understatement, I guess, as I was actually feeling rather orange!" which made them all roar with laughter as they tramped companionably back to the house.

Despite their tiredness the boys were very keen to hear what McDragon thought about their adventure so as soon as they reached the cottage their backpacks were dumped at the foot of the stairs Peter asked his dad if they could go to the shore and see if the otter was anywhere in sight. The answer was affirmative so long as they weren't too long because the stew and jacket potatoes would be ready soon.

As the lads approached the dragon rocks they were both very pleasantly surprised to see that there were now two big dragons sitting side by side. The old dragon seer, Effel, looking rather weary with her head resting between her front feet, must have arrived while they were out and there were huge ruts in the shingle on the beach which ended in a big pile up near the rocks at the back. Obviously, she'd had another one of her rather interesting landings. Her pink frillio was under her chin giving her nose a nice glow as it worked its healing magic on her.

After the dragon greeting hum, Peter launched into the story about the trip to the hidden island. When he reached the part about McMuran and the witch arriving, McDragon looked very thoughtful.

"Seraphina kept me cloaked in dragon magic so they wouldn't spot me – it did feel odd, but it worked a treat!"

He related all that had been said about the witch's hunt for a tiny dragon and that she had her squawkins searching for Brenda's lair. Then when he got to the part about the dragon etchings appearing on the walls and the one dragon picture that was a twin of Finnia, even Effel raised her huge head as if to take more of the tale in.

A "Hurrumph!" stopped Peter for a moment but then he continued, "When I touched the etching of the tiny dragon on the lectern top, the floor slid away as I was spiralled slowly downwards to end up between two lit passageways either side of me.

Biffy called out to me at that point, so I couldn't go any further and I panicked for a moment but then had the forethought to brush my finger across the tiny dragon on the lectern top and was fortunately carried back up to the turret room. As I was on the way up, I bent over to look down each of the passageways and …" his voice rose excitedly, "they each had pictures of dragons lining the walls! What's more McDragon, the castle on that island looked very much like the one that was shown in the etchings in the Dragon seer's cave – what remains of it, of course!"

"Very interesting," Effel murmured, her head still resting on top of the lovely pink and healing frillio. "Very interesting indeed!"

Before he could stop them, more words burst out of Peter's mouth, "I want to go back! I feel that I have to go back!"

The black dragon stared at him intently while Biffy stood there with his mouth dropping open with shock.

"That'd be lunatic!"

"My bones or maybe it's actually my dragon kin senses tell me that there is something there that I have to find something, something important!"

"Oh…, well," Biffy sighed loudly, "I suppose I can't let you go on your own but, to be honest, the thought of climbing those steps again doesn't fill me with any joy."

"I wasn't able to explore the lower areas of the castle once Rory got back, because he wanted to show us around some more and he didn't leave us alone again."

The big black dragon made a hmmmming noise as if he was pondering on the problem. Then he looked at Effel.

"Seer Effel, will you be recovered enough to fly to the Dragon seers' cave tomorrow? There may be something which has been foreseen which could aid us before we venture to this new island with Petersmith."

Peter felt his heart leap at that, it sounded rather as if McDragon would be with him when he revisited the castle and that was so reassuring.

"That sounds like a good plan, McDragon,"

Effel was nodding thoughtfully, looking sideways at Biffy as she did. Peter knew exactly what she was thinking! There was no way she'd be able to carry Biffy on her back and his heart sank as he guessed what the option would be – he'd have to go with Effel and that was not an enticing thought because her flying was dreadfully erratic and it made his tummy feel rather bad.

McDragon must have understood Effel's thought processes as well.

"Master Biffy, as Seer Effel has travelled so far to get here, I believe it would be too much for her to carry you or Petersmith all the way to the caves so, I'm very sorry, but on this occasion, we won't be able to take you with us."

Biffy looked a bit disappointed at that but then he perked up and said, "At least that means I can sleep in longer. That would be good!"

CHAPTER EIGHTEEN

Sleep came easily to the boys, particularly Peter whose adventures had quite worn him out, but he awoke the next morning feeling totally refreshed. When he sneaked a look into Alice's room Biffy was snoring away, lying on his back and Peter left him to it while he went to get washed and dressed.

As he raced down to the dragon rocks, his usual apple clutched in his hand, he was filled with excitement. He was going to fly with the dragons again! He was so very lucky. What would the Dragon seers' cave show them today?

The dragon welcoming song being over McDragon warmed Peter up by huffing over him. As in previous times, it was an effort for Peter to scramble up to his lofty perch at the base of McDragon's neck and he had to have help from the black and gold dragon's snout to give him a shove as his dodgy hand didn't grip quite as well as a fully able-bodied person's hand did. The scales by his knees locked down to keep him safely in place and then they lifted straight up from the ground and were on their way.

Peter looked back and tried not to snigger as he saw Effel's rather ungainly take off. She didn't quite manage it the way McDragon had and he felt a bit mean that he found it so amusing seeing as it was quite a feat for her to get airborne.

"Are we in dragon time, McDragon?"

"Of course, Petersmith! Don't worry, you will be back in time to break your fast and your dad will not be any the wiser of your absence."

The journey to the Dragon seers' cave was a familiar one to Peter and although he kept an eye out for the evil squawkins who'd often attacked them on past journeys this time there was no sign of them.

"I forgot something important that I overheard, McDragon. McMuran told the witch that he had diaries from one of his ancestors who had a theory that Arletta had come from the island where the turret room is. He believes that somewhere in the diaries it will show how she was lured to his own island, where her bones now rest."

"That is a worrying thought, Petersmith. I know he managed to entrap me somehow but to have a way to capture any dragon he desires is of great concern. We can only hope that the Dragon seers will alert us if he finds details of the necessary spell."

Out of the corner of his eye Peter saw something large coming up behind them and he called out,

"What ho, Seraphina – it's good to see you!"

"Likewise, young Petersmith."

McDragon had asked Peter to get in touch with Seraphina via her dragon scale and for her to meet them at the Dragon seers' caves, bringing Finnia with her. Peter had felt a warm glow when he realised that he'd get to see the tiny dragon again.

He looked far below them spotting a pair of eagles circling and realised that the dragons had reached the point where they would soon be diving towards the mouth of the caves. He drew his legs tightly against McDragon and bent low over the spiny long neck – in the past McDragon's entrance had been a bit haphazard and he didn't want to get knocked by the rocks on either side of them. As it happened the huge dragon made a perfect landing onto the ledge which led into the cave and then pounded along the rocky floor, his talons making a scrapping noise until he gradually slowed to a stop.

"Best landing yet, McDragon!" Peter told him.

"Hurrumph!" was the response.

Seraphina's entrance was, of course, perfect.

Effel's arrival was as expected, all over the place, after all she was very, very, old and flying and landing did not come naturally to her any more, although Peter did have a sneaking suspicion that perhaps those things have never been her forte. He'd never know if he was right. Her wings slapped against the walls as she entered, dragon blood dripping down onto the floor making her slip from side to side. Once she eventually came to a halt, the smell of singed wings surrounded them as she used her spit to close up the multiple wounds.

As soon as the dragon scales released his knees Peter dismounted carefully. Looking down beneath his feet were the deep marks many dragons had made over hundreds and thousands of years. When he straightened up much to his delight and surprise something leapt onto his shoulders and Finnia curled her long tail comfortably around his neck.

"Hello, little one! I've missed you!"

She touched his cheek as if to say she felt the same way.

They set off down the tunnel in single file, Peter first with Finnia on his shoulders followed closely by McDragon – the lights along the tunnel flickered in front of them showing them the way. Effel was last.

Although he was quite aware that the magical pictures altered depending on who had come to view them nonetheless Peter gasped when he saw the first etching – a new one to him. He was astounded to see a wizard standing in front of what appeared to be the very same lectern that Peter had found in the turret room – his wand was at the ready as he studied the big book lying in front of him. The next sketch showed the wand being waved in the air – pointing at an object which was on the floor. He peered at it more closely, as did Finnia who gave a huge jolt, almost tumbling from Peter's neck. The "something" the wizard was aiming at was a small stone dragon, in fact it could have been a replica of Finnia!

"Oh my!" Peter exclaimed as McDragon's huge head reached down to look at what had so stunned Petersmith.

After standing for some time in front of the etching, McDragon turned to Finnia, "That explains a great deal!"

They moved on and there was the self-same wizard with his pointy hat – the very top of it bending over slightly. This time although he was again in front of the lectern with the wand resting next to the book the difference was that nestled around his neck was a small dragon, exactly the same colour as Finnia.

Peter could feel the tiny dragon trembling with excitement as she stared and stared at her look-a-like.

"There, young Finnia!" Effel's voice came to them as she too examined the picture, "It seems that your forebears were made by the same wizard who brought us dragons to life!"

Finnia puffed out a little sigh just as Peter realised what the picture meant.

"So, the dragonas were made to become wizard's companions?"

"It certainly does seem that way, Petersmith, and possibly they came into being before us dragons," Effel responded.

They continued down the tunnel stopping and staring every so often at the etchings of the wizard war where the dragons and gargoyles were brought alive. It reminded Peter of the conversation that McMuran had had with the witch woman when they were on the island.

McDragon had proudly told him on their first visit to the Dragon seers' caves that the dragons remained just as they had been when they were first brought to life, unlike the gargoyles which had later become the hateful shrieking and dangerous squawkins.

"McDragon! See those battlements where the stone dragons are being magicked to life?"

"Yes, Petersmith," the big dragon's voice echoed down the tunnel.

"Well, I was right, that is exactly where Rory took us," and when Peter studied it he could see that only a few of the stone dragons remained, in fact, there were four left in situ, exactly the number that had been there only yesterday.

"I wonder why that number…" Peter mused.

"Maybe he ran out of time, Petersmith, or maybe he wanted to leave something to protect the castle in future."

While Peter stared at the castle, trying to fix in his mind what it had looked like before its collapse, there was a loud groan and Effel crashed to the floor, her head and neck stretched out in front of her and her eyes glazing over.

"Is it a seizure or do you think she is having a vision," Peter felt quite panicky – he was quite attached to Effel and couldn't bear to think of something bad happening to her.

Effel's eyes began to roll rather scarily in their sockets, but it was a huge relief to see that she was still breathing. He'd been with Effel when her seer's foresight had happened before but this was much scarier.

"Lucky we're in dragon time," he thought to himself, but then his tummy rumbled loudly – it never seemed to appreciate dragon time. Selfishly, he rather hoped she would recover soon because he had no idea how he was going to return home with her body blocking their escape route.

At that very moment, Effel opened her eyes very wide and looking quite petrified she uttered the words, "Danger! Much danger!!"

CHAPTER NINETEEN

"So, what happened next?!" Biffy asked as they followed Peter's dad along the top of the cliffs to the car later that morning.

"Well, she was out for the count for what seemed a very long time and it was lucky I had an apple with me for the flight back, because I was starving!" Peter stopped speaking when he realised his dad had waited for them at a corner and was now nearly beside them.

"I'll tell you later," he whispered before asking what they were planning to go and see.

"I thought we'd just go exploring. I'm going to take us past the old whaling station – it would be good for you to see a bit of real Outer Hebridean history. We passed it the first time we were in Harris but for some reason I forgot to point it out to you."

"Do they still use it?" Peter felt rather sick to the stomach of the thought of poor whales being killed.

"No, it closed down years ago."

"Good! What will we be having for lunch, dad?"

"I'm rather surprised you can think of food so soon after eating that big breakfast!" his dad chortled, "It must be the sea air getting to you again. Don't worry, I've brought some Scotch pies with us, some more of Biffy's cake, and apples and in case you get desperate, some chocolate. Trust me, you won't starve!"

The smell of bacon had welcomed Peter as he'd approached the cottage after his flight with the dragons. The aroma had been quite enticing and it left Peter almost drooling when he opened the door leading into the kitchen. He was not overly surprised to see Biffy in charge of the stove, flipping bacon over and readying another frying pan which was set to receive some eggs.

"Just in time, Dragon boy!" Biffy grinned, "Amazing isn't it that you know exactly when to come back to eat?!" he grinned knowingly.

Breakfast had tasted as wonderful as it had smelled, and Peter had soon gobbled his up following it down quickly with toast and marmalade.

It wasn't long after that that the three of them had set off to the car.

Much to Peter's dismay Finnia had opted to remain with the old big dragons – it seemed that she had an increasing desire for their company which made Peter a little sad knowing his time with her was becoming shorter and shorter. There were so few days left before they returned home.

The remnants of the old whaling station held his gaze as they drove past it – all that was left was a tall brick-built tower. Close by was a small harbour where a few RIBs and fishing boats were moored.

Biffy borrowed Peter's binoculars to look closer at the remains of the building.

By the time they returned to the cottage they all felt they had had a good time. They'd picnicked by a burn, watching the water looking quite stunning as it tumbled quite rapidly over dark grey and black rocks. Then on to Huishnish where the beach was covered by beautiful large egg-shaped stones. Biffy hadn't been there before, and he quite enjoyed piling stones up on top of one another to make a kind of cairn, but it also gave Peter an opportunity to at last bring Biffy up to date on the dragon situation.

"Effel couldn't quite remember much of her vision when she was out for the count, so McDragon suggested we leave her where she'd collapsed and that we'd go to the very end of the etchings where, lo and behold, some new pictures had appeared. Dragon magic is so very amazing! You were in one of the pictures with me."

"Me? What did it show?"

"We were back at the castle ruins, and in fact we were actually in the tower room together with Finnia. There was no sign of Rory, but we were both looking rather petrified."

"Could you see what it was that we were shocked about?"

"No…but when we spoke to Effel she said that although it would be very dangerous it was essential that we went back to the island. She was rather woozy at that point so McDragon is hoping that she will remember a bit more once she is back to full health again. The plan is that we fly there tomorrow morning, regardless of whether Effel has remembered anything or not and we just have to hope that McMuran and the witch don't have the same idea because we definitely don't want to run into them!"

"Too right we don't!"

"OK, Dragon boy," Biffy said rather hesitantly as they made their way down to meet McDragon and Effel, "but what did the other etchings show?"

"That's a bit of a mystery really because the last couple were totally blurred – Finnia bristled when she saw them, almost as if she could see something no-one else could but although McDragon did question her, she didn't give him any clues about them."

* * *

Later that day as soon as the dragon greeting song was over the two big dragons, one tiny dragona, a Dragon kin boy and a non-magical lad sat together for a pow wow on the rocks. Even though she was a dragon whose moods were difficult to read it was quite clear to Peter that Effel was exhausted – how on earth she'd managed to fly herself back to the beach was a mystery, but somehow, she had done it. Her head was low and even her spines running down her long neck were floppy.

"Seer Effel," Peter said politely, "shall I bring your frillio to you to help heal you?"

"Good thinking, Petersmith," she answered weakly and he ran to where he could see the lovely pink vibrant thing resting beside a small pool of water. When he picked it up with his dodgy hand the gentle pink fronds softened and slowly a pink tinge coloured his fingers as he pushed his fingers into it. It gave his hand a soft warm feeling.

He took it over to Effel and she lifted her head to enable him to place it carefully under her gnarled chin.

"I fear, Petersmith, that there is some urgency for you to return to the island. You will have to search for something that is very important to all dragons. All I know is that it is related to the wizard who created the dragonas."

McDragon looked at the boys, "I will take you tomorrow, Petersmith and Haribald d'Ness will transport young Master Biffy. Can you contact Seraphina yet again please and ask her if that will be possible, Petersmith?"

Rummaging about in his pocket for the large dragon scale he replied, "Of course, McDragon. I will do that immediately."

He felt a great relief that his stomach wouldn't have to cope with flying with Effel, although looking at the state she was in now meant that unless a miracle happened, she definitely wouldn't be with them.

CHAPTER TWENTY

The early morning departure took place as planned with Biffy sitting atop Haribald and Peter astride McDragon, his knees nestled beneath the big dragon scales which had locked down to hold him in place. Finnia was tucked safely inside his jacket to stop her being blown away. Even if she could fly it was unlikely that she'd have managed it in the wind and rain which was currently pelting down on top of them.

A surprise was in store for them before they took off as a rather bedraggled and wet crow swept towards them cawing loudly. He fluttered down and settled on Haribald d'Ness' neck fixing his beady eyes on Biffy. Biffy stared right back looking a bit awkward. The crow had a stripe of white down one wing.

"Archie!" Peter called, "Were you planning on coming with us?"

The crow answered with a loud squawk tilting his head as he continued to look at Biffy. Biffy shrugged and spoke to Peter, "What does he want, Dragon boy?"

"My guess is that he wants to get inside your jacket, firstly to get warm and secondly to rest after his flight."

"How can you know all that?"

"Well, it kind of makes sense to me." Archie crowed his agreement and hopped a little closer to Biffy, who rather hesitantly put out his arm and unzipped his jacket. The large black bird snuggled up as soon as he was put against Biffy's chest and Biffy did his coat up as much as he was able.

Peter laughed when he heard Biffy ask the crow quietly if he would like some cake because Biffy himself always found that would help him get over his tiredness.

Despite the wet, Peter soon relaxed into the enjoyment of the flight and he let his mind wander. He'd had a chat with Spit the previous night.

They'd begun their conversation with the usual, "How do you do?" and Peter could almost feel Spit's rumble of laughter as they spoke.

Spit had got over his sulks about not being able to visit the Dragon seers' cave. He'd spent the day fishing which made him realise how lovely it was to be able to feed whenever he wanted to and no longer had to rely on McMuran's sidekick, Slider, bringing him the sloppy food that he'd had to eat while he was trapped within the wizard's magic bubble.

Spit had been as intrigued as Peter at what was so important and hidden in the ruined castle. He was also rather concerned about the safety of his human friend. As they talked Peter could see and hear Archie who had been flying and squawking quite near to Spit's head.

Before they'd ended their conversation, Spit warned Peter to be on the lookout for trouble while he was at the castle and Peter had promised to do just that. They'd ended with the usual "Over and out!" which always amused them both. It was rather jolly having a dragon friend.

As he flew, Peter spoke briefly again to an exuberant Spit. Spit was feeling rather pleased with himself because he'd asked his good friend, Archie, to go to Petersmith, which explained the late arrival of the crow. Spit had had a gut feeling that Archie might be of some help to the boys and Peter teased him, suggesting that maybe he would become a seer like Effel. In his head he saw Spit roll his eyes heavenwards at that thought.

Their destination came into view on the horizon and McDragon made sure that they went the long way around to avoid passing over McMuran's island in case there were any squawkins on guard. The second island was shrouded in mist and Peter had to help guide McDragon towards it but once they'd navigated through to the clear sky in the centre McDragon made a low dive across the top of the ruined castle before performing a very skilful landing in the small clearing in front of the turret.

There was no sign of the witch or wizard on either island, which was a great relief to both Peter and McDragon.

Once released Peter slid to the ground and McDragon immediately took off to give Haribald the space to land and let Biffy slide rather unceremoniously down onto the ground. The two dragons then flew high into the still rainy sky circling way above the boys.

As soon as Peter was on his feet Finnia wriggled out of his jacket and settled herself around his shoulders, sniffing loudly with her nose in the air and then, rather like a setter on point, stared across at the four stone dragons seemingly on guard outside the turret room.

Biffy brushed himself off and the boys made their way to the foot of the steps, clambering over fallen masonry as they did. Finnia's gaze remained locked on the stone dragons and once Peter arrived next to them, she leapt from his shoulders to examine each dragon up close. Peter could have sworn he saw the eyes of the first one blink when Finnia was nose to nose with it, but then he shrugged his shoulders guessing it was his imagination getting carried away.

"Biffy, can you stay on guard while I go inside?"

"Will do Dragon boy!" There was a squawking sound from inside of Biffy's coat – it seemed that Archie was very keen to get free. He hopped out as soon as the coat was undone and fluttered up to settle on Biffy's shoulder and much to the bigger lad's surprise, gave a small peck to Biffy's ear as if to say, "Thank you."

The boys looked up and despite the rain it was comforting to see the two big dragons circling above them using their keen hearing to listen out for the sound of a whistle from below which would indicate there was danger. They would then race down to snatch the boys to safety.

Peter squeezed himself through the gap in the window waiting impatiently for Finnia who was still peering at the stone dragons. She touched her nose to the last one and Peter thought it was a shame he couldn't converse with her as he would have loved to have known what was going through her head at that moment.

At long last she leapt through the gap and landed back on his shoulders pinning her gaze immediately onto the dragon that was etched into the ceiling. As they both stood there admiring the huge dragon, the pictures on the smooth walls began to materialise and the little dragona hissed as her vision focussed on the one that looked the same as her.

"Amazing!" Peter breathed.

Aware that time was ticking away he crossed over to the lectern, running his hand across its surface until he felt the tiny dragon scratched there. As before he pressed it with his forefinger and the stone slab they were standing on began its slow twisting descent. The lectern went down with them.

Finnia curled herself tightly around his neck as the two of them felt themselves moving towards the depths of the unknown – the magical lights on the walls glowing below them.

Once they were at the bottom Peter gave some thought to the etchings in the Dragon seers' cave and how the castle had looked when it was complete. Darkened corridors disappeared off to the right and left of them. Which way should they go?

"Let's toss and let fate decide for us," Peter suggested and fished into his pocket where he had a twenty pence coin. "Heads, we go left and tails, we go right."

The coin spun in the air, light catching it until it tinkled on the ground. Peter bent down to see what the decision was to be.

"Heads it is!" he announced. Immediately he took his first step into the lefthand passageway, the magical lights lit up showing them the way forward and it was only a matter of a seconds before they stepped into a small empty circular room. The walls were smooth and very pleasant to touch as Peter skimmed his hand along them, dragon etchings emerging as he did.

Finnia's small nose prodded his neck.

"What is it?"

She pushed her snout against the wall's surface just above his hand and very slowly and smoothly the wall slid away and watery sunlight filtered in.

"A door! So, this is how the wizards of old entered the castle!"

CHAPTER TWENTY-ONE

"Oi! Biffy!," Peter shouted when they were standing in the open.

"Yeah!"

Peter stuck his head around the edge of the wall until he could see Biffy standing guard at the top of the steps. Peter waved at him.

"Get back here!" he called.

Biffy took his time reaching them and as he waited Peter had the foresight to try closing and reopening the door before his friend arrived. They would have had a huge problem if Biffy wasn't able to exit through the doorway because there was no way he would be able to squash his body through the window in the turret room.

Archie fluttered down and sat on Biffy's shoulder as the boy's face cracked into a huge beam when he saw what confronted him.

Peter hesitated for a moment before reaching across to stroke the crow gently and asking, "Archie, would you be able to keep look out for us please?" The crow cawed and flew back up into the air.

Biffy was amazed when Peter stroked the tactile smooth walls which lined the very plain entrance way and touched the almost unnoticeable tiny dragon etching to enable the door to slide smoothly back in place. They walked back along the short corridor, Peter marching quite confidently until they reached the magical lift and then he moved forward until they finally stepped into another small circular room. This one had stone shelving running along the walls which were empty apart from the one immediately in front of them. They both walked across to it and Peter's breath whooshed out as resting on the shelf was a large purple covered book.

Finnia gave a small hiss of delight, almost skipping from her resting place on his shoulders to land on top of the book. She nudged at the cover and immediately a stunning picture appeared in full colour. It was not just any dragon, but a small dragona just like her!

"Wow! Oh, my goodness!" whispered Peter. "This must be what Effel must have meant us to find as there is nothing else here at all!" Touching it gave him a tingle in the back of his neck as he picked it up and tucked it under his arm. Finnia scampered back to her usual resting place around his neck.

The lights in the room stuttered and dimmed once the book was taken from the shelving, which reinforced the feeling that there was nothing else to look at in the room. Peter led the way back to the step beneath the entrance to the turret room. He stood on the flat stone waiting for Biffy to join him. Biffy shuffled forward rather hesitantly and braced himself as Peter's fingers brushed over the dragon etching and the lectern and step began to revolve lifting them up towards the turret room.

Once all movement had ceased, and the stone slab returned to its original position showing none of the depths below, Biffy crossed over to the walls to look at the etchings shown there. He stopped at the one showing the dragona, his gaze alternating from the picture and then back to Finnia, time and time again.

"It could be you, Finnia," he told her.

Peter placed the beautiful book onto the lectern in front of him and nearly fell over with shock as a wand appeared immediately next to it.

He stared and stared at it and then couldn't resist touching it rather reverently, as he did the dragona picture on the front began to glow rather magnificently encouraging him to thumb the pages carefully. They felt unlike anything he had touched before, papery but also soft and almost velvety – just how he might have imagined vellum would be like.

The first page showed a wizard in a long gown who had his arm outstretched and was pointing his wand at something on the floor in front of him. Peter moved his head a little closer and drew in a deep breath – the recipient of the magic coming from the wand was a small stone dragon and there were words written on the opposite page. Peter opened his mouth about to try and say them when there was a frantic cawing outside followed by a loud cackle of glee. The witch!! She was here!

"Found you!" she screamed in delight, her big nose wobbling slightly as her head appeared at the window.

"You! I should have known!" she turned to face something outside and shrieked, "Get in there and bring me that book!!! Now!!!"

"And you! Kill them and get the dragon!"

With a huge thrust of air once the witch's head moved out of the way two small gargoyle-like squawkins followed one another into the room. They both had evil gleams on their faces. One headed straight towards Peter and the other flew at Biffy.

Peter slammed the book shut and pushed it onto the floor, instinctively grabbing the wand resting beside it. His arm reached up for Finnia but she wasn't there!

Archie burst into the room immediately behind the squawkins and arrowed towards the squawkin going for Biffy. He thrust his long beak into the squawkin's misshapen ear and it screamed in pain, shaking its head and backing away as Archie crashed to the floor. Biffy threw himself over the big bird to bravely try and protect it.

Before the other squawkin could reach Peter, seemingly out of nowhere, Finnia shot towards it and a stream of fire fiercely rushed into its ugly face until it fled back out through the window knocking into the witch and shrieking so loudly that Peter had to put his fingers into his ears.

Peter's focus of attention moved back to Finnia but he was too late, still shaking its head the other squawkin recovered sufficiently to snatch her up in its nasty poisonous claws and beat a hasty retreat towards the window.

Without thinking Peter clutched the wand very tightly in his dodgy hand and pointed it at the squawkin. He wiggled the wand and to his immense surprise a spurt of light shot from it and touched Finnia's small head just as the squawkin escaped through the window opening. There was a flash from the little dragon and the squawkin nearly dropped her just as Peter realised he had turned her to stone!

"Finnia! No! No! No!" Peter shouted as he started to propel himself to the gap but as he reached it, with a clap of hands high above her head the witch and the two squawkins disappeared into nothingness, Finnia with them.

"Finnia!!!" screamed a very distraught Peter, "Finnia!!!" and dropping the wand he threw himself down beating his fists on the ground.

CHAPTER TWENTY-TWO

The pair of boys who'd trudged from the beach to the cottage had their heads bowed low – each of them looking very sad indeed.

Before they reached the front door, Biffy whispered, "We need to put on a brave face for your dad or he'll be asking some questions we can't answer, Dragon boy."

Peter nodded but all he could really think about was poor Finnia. Where was she? Was she injured at all? And the biggest question of all, how on earth were they going to rescue her?

Immediately after the witch had vanished, McDragon had landed full of fire and ready for battle, Haribald immediately behind him. They had heard the kerfuffle that had taken place too late for them to be of use during the fight.

Peter called across to let them know he was going to let Biffy out of the hidden doorway. The bigger boy cradled a still very whoozy Archie in his arms as they waited for the stone holding the lectern to revolve and take them below. Once Biffy had left the castle, Peter checked the room which had the shelves on it, but there was still nothing to be seen there so he returned to the turret room and clambered out the window to join Biffy and the dragons who were waiting for him by the broken slabs in front of the castle.

The boys very quickly related everything that had happened, Peter choking on the words as they tumbled from his mouth, tears streaming down his cheeks and Biffy interjecting from time to time to add his views to the tale.

"Petersmith, it sounds as if there was nothing you could have done to prevent this from happening." McDragon had told them reassuringly. "The Dragon seers realised somehow that you had to return to find the book and keep it out of the witch's nasty hands. You must take it with you to keep it safe, just in case she should come back here. As far as the wand is concerned, as it materialised when you needed it and has not disappeared again you must take that too because it must be a pair with the book and you may need the two of them to try to reverse the spell and return Finnia to life. Study the book carefully so you are prepared to do just that."

Peter squeezed himself back through the window crossing immediately to where he had flung the wizard's book for safety on the floor. To his amazement it was sitting closed on top of the lectern and what was more surprising was that tucked down the spine was the wand. How on earth had that happened – he certainly hadn't done that?! McDragon must be totally correct and they belonged together.

As soon as he picked up the book, he felt that tingle in his neck and looked down at the cover. The picture of what could almost be Finnia had gone. He raised his eyebrows, thinking that dragon magic or rather wizard magic could be very unsettling sometimes.

With the book and wand zipped up safely inside his backpack Peter took one look around the room. Would he ever return here? As his gaze settled on the etchings on the wall they faded into nothingness, almost as if they knew he would be leaving. The large dragon on the ceiling also disappeared. Would it all come back if he returned to the castle in the future? He had no idea but at least he felt that it was better that should McMuran or the witch come back there would be nothing for them to see.

On their return flight to the cottage Peter asked "How can we rescue Finnia, McDragon? Is there a way? I can't bear to think of her in the clutches of the witch!"

"We will most certainly try, laddie. As the magic from the wand has returned her to stone – I certainly hope that will make it very difficult for the witch to try and control her."

"Poor Finnia!"

"Petersmith, dinna fash yersel, as the Scots say, which I believe means, don't worry. We will see if Seer Effel has remembered more of her vision." Archie reached up from where he had been stashed inside Peter's jacket and pecked his cheek softly as if to reassure him too. The crow had opted to go with Peter on their trip back to Harris and Peter felt somewhat comforted by the warmth of the bird next to him.

"But… McDragon how was Finnia able to fly and snort fire? She showed no signs of being able to do that before."

"She spent her time with us dragons wisely. She knew that breathing fire was going to be essential to her and although it is something instinctive to all dragons, sometimes we need to learn to look deep inside ourselves to find the magic that will do that. Your friend Spit asked her if she would like to learn to fly and because he is fairly new at it himself, he was actually the best dragon to show her. It took a lot of determination from her to pick up these skills in the short time she had allotted to her."

Effel had been waiting for them impatiently when they finally landed by McDragon's rocks, it looked like she had been using her magical pink frillio to aid her recovery because it was lying very close by and her snout still had the hint of a pink glow to it. She was a lot perkier than when they'd left her.

Dragon greeting hum over they had related everything that had transpired on the island.

"That explains a lot…" Effel had murmured thoughtfully closing her big eyes, "I could not see what was to happen but, I knew it would be dangerous. I have however remembered my vision and, Petersmith, it is my belief that you will be the one to rescue Finnia. Meanwhile, McDragon, Haribald d'Ness and I will give great thought to the best way to help you."

"Seer Effel?"

She looked at him gravely, "Yes, Petersmith?"

"Should… should we let Brenda know that there is a problem?"

"Hmm…, McDragon, what do you think?" Effel asked.

"That might be a sensible thing to do, Petersmith. Yes, I believe you should do so."

The boys were rather uncomfortable but, as previously arranged with Brenda, Peter raised his terrible singing voice as loudly as he could – Biffy put his fingers in his ears and even McDragon winced at the sound. Once it was finished they waited for the sign. It took a long time to arrive but at long last some clouds floated above them in the shape of a dragon – but this time the dragon had grey tears falling from the gap in the white clouds formed to look like an eye.

"Oh dear! Poor Brenda!" Peter felt even sadder than before.

"It is not your fault Petersmith – remember this path has already been written for Finnia. You could not have changed it. There will be a reason why the dragona needs to be with the witch but only time will tell the why of it. Please keep your chin up!" which had made Peter smile as that was one of his mum's expressions.

* * *

"It's lucky I thought we'd have just porridge for breakfast today boys – what on earth has happened to your appetites?" Peter's dad smiled at them. Amazingly, even Biffy was very subdued and off his food, something that Peter had never seen happen before.

"Sorry dad, maybe it's because my stomach is feeling sad that this is nearly our last day." That was about the best that Peter could come up with as an answer.

"Well, I hope your appetites are going to return by lunch time because I thought that maybe we could go to Leverburgh and visit the Butty Bus for some squid and chips. Biffy hasn't been there before. What do you think lads? Is that a good plan? We could buy some of those lovely scallops from that fisherman again, so we can have a very special last night dinner tomorrow."

"That sounds amazing, Mr Smith," Biffy answered for them both. He knew that Peter was struggling to show enthusiasm for anything.

In the car on the way to Leverburgh Peter gloomily stared out at the passing scenery. The rain had stopped for the time being and he could now see the small lochs with their brown peaty water and the rugged landscape where grey and black rocks protruded amongst very rough grass and heather. Peter always thought if one landed on the moon it might look like this.

Every so often there were peat bricks stacked neatly on top of one another close to where they'd been dug from straight sided ruts in the ground.

Water lapped into the various coves they passed, some with small boats bobbing about at their moorings.

Eventually they turned into the harbour car park. There were a few cars waiting for the ferry which was just backing up to its position in front of the ramp.

They all stretched themselves thankfully once they were out of the car. It hadn't been a particularly long drive, but it was still nice to stand up. Biffy sniffed the air appreciatively as he smelled frying and looked across past the ferry to the restaurant/bar that was there.

"Is that where we're going?" he asked.

"No lad, even closer than that!" Peter's dad answered pointing in the opposite direction. Biffy smiled when he turned – there stood the Butty Bus.

Fortunately for them, the ferry was about to leave so they were the only customers inside the small single decker bus. Stools were arrayed on both sides of it with narrow counters above them. There was just enough room for people to walk down the middle towards the frying area.

"Well boys, what takes your fancy? Have you got your appetites back yet?" Peter's dad had asked them.

Biffy was the first to answer, "What's Cullen Skink?" he asked, "And, how do you make it?"

* * *

The following morning Haribald was waiting beside McDragon and Effel, which meant that Biffy could join Peter on his last trip to see Spit. A pow wow was to take place once they arrived.

Despite feeling very melancholy about Finnia Peter still enjoyed the flight on McDragon. What's more he was really looking forward to talking to Spit face to face, something they hadn't had much time for on this visit. Archie had opted to travel with Biffy, whom Peter could see was feeding him small pieces of fruit cake. As far as they could tell the crow had recovered completely from his ordeal.

To Peter's delight Spit flew out and joined them for the last part of their journey, obviously equally keen to meet up with his human friend again. On arrival McDragon landed quite neatly in the open space on the island and once Peter had dismounted, Haribald began his descent. Spit whizzed above their heads and some way off in the distance Peter spied Effel bringing up behind them in her usual erratic wobbly manner. As soon as Haribald had moved out of the way Spit set himself down and then careered towards Petersmith, looking rather pleased with himself.

"How do you do, Spit?" Peter enquired.

"Very well thank you, Petersmith" Spit responded and skidding to a halt, he lifted his front foot as if to shake hands, giggling as he did. That set Peter off and soon the two of them were laughing, Biffy standing a little way apart watching the two friends greeting one another. Archie had been released from his cosy nest inside Biffy's coat and was flapping around Spit's head.

Spit braced himself and began to swish his tail looking as if he was ready to bundle Peter to the ground, which is what they had always done in the past, but Peter stopped him saying, "You've grown so much Spit that if you want to rough play with me you'll likely break some of my bones!"

"Sorry, Petersmith, I nearly forgot. I'm just so very happy to see you!"

"Likewise! And you have my thanks for having the forethought in sending Archie to help us – that was a master stroke!"

Spit preened himself, looking very proud at the praise from his good friend, just as Biffy suddenly shouted a warning, "Look out! Effel's landing!"

Peter and Spit rushed out of the way, Effel's landings were notoriously bad and as expected she crashed down and slid across the ground before ending up in a heap against some rocks. She struggled onto her haunches and shook her big head from side to side.

"I thought I might have got a bit better at this by now, but obviously I need more practice!"

The boys stifled their giggles not wanting to upset her in any way. She was older than the hills and deserved their respect.

Spit commenced the greeting song and the boys joined him just as Seraphina and Popple added their voices to the dragon music.

CHAPTER TWENTY-THREE

There was silence in the car as they waited for the ferry to arrive to deliver them back to Uig for their homeward journey and even when they reached land at the other end not even the sight of the harbour seals excited either boy.

The night before they'd shared a lovely meal which Peter's dad and Biffy had prepared. That was after Peter's dad's usual struggle to open the scallop shells when he'd had to apologise for the bad language that was used as he wrestled with the pesky mollusks. The knack of it still eluded him, despite having had yet another lesson from the scallop diver when they'd bought them. The scallops fought hard to keep their shells clammed shut but by sheer perseverance he finally succeeded and scraped away the frilly gelatinous glob which surrounded the beautiful white and orange scallops inside.

At bedtime Peter and Biffy had sat on the edge of Peter's bed talking quietly about the pow wow they'd had with the dragons.

Popple's small head rested against Peter's thigh as the discussion was taking place and he'd absentmindedly stroked her scaly forehead as he listened. Spit was on his other side trying desperately hard to contain his excitement in having not only his friend with him but also being allowed to be part of the planning process. Every so often his tail would sweep from side to side and he would bounce up and down a bit.

At last it was decided that Haribald and McDragon would make the long journey to meet the boys near Petersmith's home. The flight would have to take place in stages, with the dragons landing wherever they could find a lake that would provide some fish for sustenance. They would meet Peter and Biffy in the small park that was not far from Peter's home.

Shortly after that had been agreed upon, Spit had caused a big dust storm around them when his tail just couldn't contain itself – he was so very proud, proud because he had been tasked with being the key dragon as far as communication was concerned. Peter had left the dragon scale that Seraphina had given him with Haribald in order to help Haribald and Seraphina keep in close touch with one another. Seraphina, in turn, would pass information on to Spit, and that would enable Peter and Spit to speak via Spit's scale. They all agreed that that was the simplest way to keep everyone in the loop.

Not one of them doubted that Finnia was to be found at the witch's cottage.

The drive back home seemed very long although they did find time to stop and wander around Fort William just to stretch their legs. There was a book shop in the town which Peter's dad particularly enjoyed. However, once they hit the motorway Peter dozed on and off and in between times he kept running their adventures through his head.

The thought of Effel raised a smile on his face at one point when he remembered their last conversation. She was going to make her permanent home part of a grassy dragon shaped promontory covered in a mass of lichen, a mere stone's throw from where McDragon's rocks were. As Effel had pointed out, that way she could more easily be a part of all the excitement that seemed to stir around their dragon kin, Petersmith. She would remain a Dragon seer but, as long as her body could cope with it, take part in any of the action.

Peter was rather hoping that the so called "action" wouldn't be dangerous – but that seemed rather a futile wish in the circumstances. Everything to do with dragons seemed to be fraught with danger and he kept wondering how a rather small young boy with a slightly disabled hand could be caught up in all the hoo-ha to do with dragons! At least Biffy would be with him on the rescue adventure.

The other matter which often passed through his head was how on earth Biffy could change from being such a bully boy into the kind person he was now? Dragon magic could be a real mystery!

At long last the car pulled up outside Biffy's house, it was quite late at night and although Biffy's parents had been made aware he would be home that night, there were no lights shining a welcome.

Biffy looked up at the dark windows and just shrugged his shoulders rummaging in his pocket for the door key.

"See you tomorrow, Biffy?" Peter asked.

"Yup, if that's OK?"

"Of course."

Peter's dad got out and carried his bag up to the front door waiting for Biffy to let himself into the dark hallway.

"Ok lad?"

"It's fine and Mr Smith… thank you so much for letting me come along. I had a great time and I really love the Isle of Harris – it's amazing!"

"My pleasure. See you soon Biffy."

Once the door closed behind the boy Peter's dad returned to the car and drove them home, where a totally different scene met them. Lights were blazing throughout the house and a very welcoming hug was waiting for both members of the Smith family.

CHAPTER TWENTY-FOUR

"Have you heard from Spit?" were the first words out of Biffy's mouth as soon as he and Peter were on their own in Peter's room the next day.

"Yes… but nothing really to report. Spit is still feeling rather excited about being given, what I would call the Dragon Communications Post. I hope he calms down once everything kicks off because we're going to need him to be on the ball."

Biffy smiled as did Peter when they both pictured the young dragon bouncing about and swishing his tail from side to side.

"He's been practising his flying and fishing in readiness for our next visit to Harris."

The smile dropped from Biffy's face.

"What's up mate?" Peter enquired.

"Well… I can't imagine your parents wanting me to come along next time. What's more have you ever wondered just how many times they'll want to return to the island? What happens if they suddenly decide to go somewhere else?"

Peter patted him on the back and said, "I've already asked if you can come with us and the answer was "Yes"," Biffy beamed back at him. "What's more dad says he has a lot more research to do on the Outer Hebrides and then he'll move on to the Inner Hebrides – not that I know quite what it is he does. Funnily enough I saw him looking at properties in the paper while we were there. I can't imagine my parents would have enough money to buy one, but we all like to dream, don't we?"

The answer was a very serious nod and Peter could only guess at what Biffy would dream about… apart from cooking.

He changed the subject. "I do hope Finnia is alright, I feel really mortified that I unwittingly turned her to stone."

"Think positive, Dragon boy! Effel believes there is a reason that Finnia had to go with the witch and also that it is written that you will rescue Finnia, so you just *have* to believe! After all, wasn't it written before that you would be the one to find Popple's Pearl and who on earth would have imagined that you would be the very one to do just that?!" Peter grinned his answer to that.

He began to empty his school bag to check that he'd actually finished all of his homework. Fortunately, he had. He repacked the bag carefully. School tomorrow and the good thing was that at least Biffy wouldn't be waiting for him with his gang in tow at the school gate ready to terrorise him as he used to.

* * *

The boys met up as they always did recently at the end of Biffy's road and ambled along together chatting aimlessly until Biffy admitted that he would feel more relaxed once this dragon business was over and done with.

"Don't tell me the cripple has made you believe in dragons too!" a voice crowed from behind them. They'd not noticed that one of the boys from their class had caught up with them.

Peter swung about and faced up to the boy. He recognised him immediately as a lesser member of Biffy's old gang.

"I don't laugh at you for being short and fat, so I'd appreciate it if you didn't call me a cripple. I can't help it that I was born like it, for the same reason you are unable to change being short!" Peter glared at the boy, who took a step backwards looking rather taken aback, a bit like a cat that had caught a mouse by the tail and found that it could bite.

He lifted both hands in the air as if to say, "Whoa!" and stepped past them and walked away quite quickly.

"Well done, Dragon boy!" Biffy gave him a pat on the back. "Well said!"

They carried on the journey to school, each deep in his own thoughts. As they walked Peter glanced up at Biffy to try and see if he could work out what his friend was thinking. He had an odd look on his face and Peter wondered if perhaps Biffy was remembering what a terror he'd been in the past.

As Peter struggled to concentrate in the physics lesson he felt a warming in his pocket and slipped his hand inside to grasp the small dragon scale.

In his head he answered, "How do you do Spit?"

He could see that Spit was dancing about, Archie zooming round and round his head as if he was excited too.

"Very well, thank you!" Spit answered and then burst out with, "They have left, Petersmith. McDragon and Haribald are on their way to you now. I will let you know when they eventually get near to you."

"That's good news," Peter responded in his head, "I'd best go now as I'm in school in a lesson at the moment – I'll contact you later on. Over and out!"

He couldn't wait to tell Biffy the news, but he'd have to wait until the break. He really needed to try and concentrate on what the physics teacher was explaining. It was different with biology, he found that easy to understand.

He felt someone's gaze on him and looked across the room at the boy who had laughed at them that morning. Peter just nodded his head with a grave expression on his face and the boy seemed to dip his chin slightly in response.

In the final break Peter rushed to find Biffy, keen to break the news to him. He found him on the other side of the playground looking across at something.

Peter followed his gaze and was surprised to see the boys from Biffy's old gang surrounding a smaller lad. The boy who was in the midst of them was the chap who had laughed at them that morning and he looked rather nervous.

"Shall we get closer and see what's going on?" Peter whispered quietly.

Biffy seemed rather worried but nevertheless he obediently followed Peter who was edging his way across the playground.

The circle of boys was pressing in even more on the shorter lad and one of the bullies pushed at his prey's shoulder, turning him sideways.

"Hey!" Peter called as he got closer. "Is there a problem?"

"Mind your own business!" a fierce voice answered.

"It's only that I need a word with… erm…" Peter couldn't remember the name at all, but Biffy whispered from behind him, "Simon."

"Simon." Peter said.

"Can't it wait until later on?" said the biggest boy turning towards him. "Oh, it's you, the cripple called Dragon boy!" and he started to laugh at what he thought was his amazing speech. The other boys with him chuckled along with him.

Peter stalked up to him and stared into his face, "As I told Simon only this morning, I am *not* a cripple and I don't appreciate being called one! Call me Dragon boy if you want, that's no skin off of my nose!"

There was a face off as the big boy peered down at Peter. Peter continued to glare at him and refused to back away, but he noticed that while everyone's attention was on him and his opponent, Simon slipped out of range and moved across the playground.

Thankfully the whistle shrilled indicating the end of the break and everyone had to stand still before being instructed to go back into the school.

"This isn't over Dragon boy! Not by a long chalk!" the bully hissed at him, giving Biffy a stare as well, before marching off into the school, his followers close behind him.

"What did you do that for, Dragon boy?" Biffy muttered, "You might have started a war there."

Peter shrugged his reply as he kept a close eye on the bully boys who were now entering the school.

"It shouldn't be allowed to happen… you know that now, don't you?"

Biffy wouldn't meet his friend's eyes even as he nodded his answer.

A random thought crossed Peter's mind as he remembered one of his mum's sayings, "What goes around comes around!". She had explained that as meaning that your sins could come back and bite you unexpectedly in the backside.

CHAPTER TWENTY-FIVE

For all his bravado, Peter kept checking they weren't being followed as they sauntered slowly back home. He wasn't at all sure what had come into his head to make him face up to what was obviously a new bully gang. Simon had sat down next to him during the next lesson and had whispered his thanks, which had made Peter feel quite good but, for all that, he wasn't quite sure how he was going to handle any trouble if it came about. For the time being though, he had more important dragon matters on his mind.

"We need to be prepared for this trip to save Finnia," he announced to Biffy, who had been very quiet all afternoon.

"What do you think we need to pack then?"

"Well, I need the wand and Spit's dragon scale of course, but I'll leave the wizard's book behind, I wouldn't want there to be any chance the witch could get her hands on it."

"Have you looked at it since you got it home?"

"Yep, a few times. It looks like gobbledegook to me."

"Have you tried holding the wand when you look at it? It's worth a go."

"Good thinking, although I'd best not say the words aloud when I do that! Who knows what could happen!"

"I suppose we'd best take some supplies in case we're away longer than expected."

Peter smothered a laugh at that, it was typical of Biffy to be thinking of his stomach.

"Lucky we'll be in dragon time – we could be away for ages and no-one miss us. You're right though, we should take food and… maybe a bottle of water each. What else?" he mused.

"Your swiss army knife and the binoculars."

"Yup! And a waterproof jacket – if you remember it did rain a lot in Wales when we were there with the school."

"Wellies or trainers?"

"Don't know what you think, but I'd vote for trainers in case we have to run at any time."

Biffy's face looked a picture as he thought of running.

Once he arrived home Peter settled down to get his homework done and then he went to his room to get organised. Although he guessed it would be a while before the dragons arrived, he needed to be ready to leave at a moment's notice.

He took out the bird book that he always had in his jacket pocket and left it on the bookshelf in his room – he wouldn't be bird spotting on this trip, that was for sure.

Binoculars, Swiss Army knife, gloves and a scarf were all laid out on the bed next to his backpack and then he slipped downstairs and filled up a water bottle and took a couple of apples from the fruit bowl. His mum wouldn't notice because he was always eating apples. He knew he could rely on Biffy to bring sandwiches and cake as those would be Biffy's priorities.

When he pulled the wand out from its hiding place at the back of one of his cupboards, he got a tingling feeling in his neck – and then at the same time there was a clear picture of the garden at the witch's cottage in his head, with mountains in the background. Was Finnia somehow sending that to him?

"Finnia! Are you OK?" Would she be able to answer? He kept his hand tightly fastened around the wand and waited. Nothing, although the picture of the garden became clearer.

"Finnia?" he whispered quietly again, but there was no answer.

After waiting a few more minutes listening to silence, he began to stash everything he needed in his bag and then slid it down a gap at the end of his bed to make sure his mum wouldn't notice it if she looked in. It was his job to keep his bedroom tidy and to put his dirty clothes in the washing bin, so he knew that really the only reason she would be in there would be to vacuum the carpet and collect the washing.

Now, did he have everything he would need? Was there anything else?

Once his school bag was packed and his clothes for the next day laid out tidily on a chair he took the opportunity to contact Spit and tell him about the witch's garden.

The two friends chatted for quite a time and Spit promised to pass on what Petersmith had seen to Seraphina and she, in turn, would relay it to McDragon. It seemed that the two big dragons were now resting overnight near a lake where they would feed their bellies with as much fish as they could catch. Their flight so far had been without any problems. Peter reminded Spit that if he and Biffy were in school when McDragon arrived then they wouldn't be able to begin their trip to the witch's cottage – first thing in the morning would probably be best, and Peter really thought that a weekend would be even more suitable but trying to explain what a weekend was to Spit didn't seem like an easy thing to do so he left it at that.

He finished with an, "Over and out, Spit! Speak to you soon."

"Peter! Dinner's on the table!"

"Coming, mum!"

CHAPTER TWENTY-SIX

As they walked to school the following morning the boys realised that the one matter they hadn't sorted out was how Peter was going to let Biffy know when the dragons had arrived and were close by.

"Not sure what to do about that, Dragon boy. I guess we'll just have to hope that you get the message early in the evening before, so you can telephone and speak to me."

"Shame we haven't a walkie talkie," Peter said and then he gave it a little more thought. "Actually, Alice and I did have a pair of them. I wonder where they are now? They could be really useful."

He put his mind to it as they walked in silence until Biffy muttered quietly out of the side of his mouth, "Look out! There may be trouble ahead!"

Peter looked up from the pavement and his heart sank to his boots as he saw a group of boys waiting for them at the crossroads.

"What's the new leader's name?" he said out of the corner of his mouth.

"Albert, I think," Biffy answered as he absentmindedly kicked a stone from the pavement into the road.

Peter drew himself up taller as he approached the gang.

"Hi, it's a nice day isn't it?" he asked them.

"Not for you it isn't!" Albert said as he stepped forward.

"Why not, what makes it different for me?"

"I do!" the big boy said menacingly.

"Not sure why," Peter answered. "What have I done to upset you?"

At that moment there was a toot on a car horn and Peter's dad's car pulled up beside them.

"Want a lift, boys? I'm going past the school."

"Thanks dad, that would be great," and Biffy and Peter piled inside.

"Do any of your friends want to come too – there's room for two more?" Peter saw that one of the boys did take a step forward and he noted which one that was, but the lad was restrained by Albert who put a hand across his chest.

"Nah… they'll enjoy the walk to school," Peter answered as he closed the door with a sigh of relief.

"Told you there'd be trouble," Biffy muttered under his breath from the back seat.

The day at school passed in the usual manner, apart from the fact that Peter kept a sharp eye out for the newly founded bully boy gang. He saw them surround a couple of other boys, and even at one point, one girl but he kept his distance and just watched. It was imperative that he didn't get into trouble before their trip – that was the priority. Even so he really felt that someone would have to do something about it and the only person who could do that would be him. He couldn't really squeal on them to the teachers because that could rebound very badly on him but… there must be some other route to take. He'd have to give it a lot of thought – but *after* the rescue of Finnia.

As soon as he was home, as he had done the previous day, after having a snack of some fruit, he settled down immediately to do his homework. He had no idea what state he was going to be in once he'd flown with the dragons, but he guessed he might be too tired to concentrate on homework afterwards and it was probably in his best interests to keep on top of it.

Once that was out of the way he began to sort through the cupboard in his bedroom where games and odds and ends were piled up. He wanted to try to find the walkie talkies but they weren't there.

Over dinner with his family Peter asked Alice if she knew what had happened to them. She thought it was incredibly funny that he wanted to use them to get in touch with Biffy and kept giggling every now and then. He didn't like to push it but he was very pleased when a little later she appeared in his doorway holding a box in her hands.

"Here they are!"

"Thanks Alice! That's kind of you to hunt them down. You know what Biffy is like, he doesn't always turn up when he says he's going to so that's why I wanted them."

"Well, have fun!" she said laughing over her shoulder as she walked towards her bedroom.

Peter took the batteries out of the handsets and replaced them with some from a game which he knew had only had the batteries put in very recently. Then he tested them out. Eureka! He ran downstairs and asked his parents if he could just nip down to Biffy's and drop something off to him – he promised to only be ten minutes or so and as it was still light outside they were happy to let him go.

Biffy's mum seemed to be down in the dumps, but that wasn't unusual. She shouted out to Biffy and returned immediately to the sitting room where he could hear the television blaring away.

Biffy came from the direction of the kitchen, flour coating his hands.

"Just baking a cake," he said and then added quietly, "Rations for our trip."

Peter smiled at that and then handed Biffy the walkie talkie.

"Alice found them for me." And he proceeded to explain how to use them. They were working perfectly.

"Now, we'll have to say, "Over and Out" like I do with Spit," Peter joked.

"Ha ha!"

Back at home, once he was bathed and ready for bed, Peter contacted Spit through the scale.

After their usual, "How do you do," he asked if Spit had any idea how McDragon and Haribald were getting along.

"They haven't been in contact today, but Seraphina isn't worried because she rather thinks they will be concentrating on making sure they don't lose their sense of where you are. Just keep a close eye on my scale in case I get in touch tonight."

As they spoke Peter could see a picture of Spit reclining on a rock on the island in the sunshine, his wings spread out either side of him. Archie was preening himself nearby, fluffing up his feathers. The sea rippled rather prettily behind them.

To take his mind off things Peter related to Spit the problem with the bully boys.

"I know it's a lot to ask, but is there any way you dragons can send magic to them to put a stop to it?"

"Petersmith, you are Dragon kin and you will find a way to deal with it in your own way. Seraphina is always impressing upon me the fact that dragon magic cannot be used willy nilly. When I asked her if she could use magic to speed up my flying strength, she told me it would be a waste of magical energy. Trust me, you'll know what to do when the time comes."

CHAPTER TWENTY-SEVEN

Peter slept with his hand under the pillow clasping the dragon scale tightly and as soon as he felt it warming in his hand he woke with a start.

"Yes, Spit!"

"McDragon asks that you meet them at dawn." Peter yawned sleepily before he answered, "OK. I'll let Biffy know. Over and out!"

It took a little while for Biffy to answer the summons from the walkie talkie but he agreed to meet Peter by the gate by the alley behind Peter's house. The park was a stone's throw from there. Once dragon time kicked in their parents wouldn't realise they'd gone anywhere. Peter felt rather bad because he normally wouldn't ever disappear without letting his parents know where he was going – somehow it was different when they were in Harris, but there was nothing for it if they had to rescue Finnia. He refused to think about what might happen if he had an accident and didn't return. To make himself feel a little better he penned a small note and put it beside his pillow telling them not to worry, he was with Biffy.

He crept out of the house rather like a burglar would, making sure the back door was closed securely before he ran down the garden and out of the gate. He could hear the puffing that would be Biffy long before his friend came into sight.

Carrying their backpacks, they walked as swiftly as they could over to the park and lo and behold the two huge dragons were waiting for them. They looked very strange in such a setting, standing next to the slide. Swings were swaying backwards and forwards in the light breeze.

"What ho, McDragon!" Peter called and then launched into his discordant dragon greeting song, Biffy joining him.

"Good morning to you too, young Petersmith and Master Biffy! I am pleased to see you are both on time, now let's be away before the dawn breaks in full."

If anyone had seen them it would have been a very odd sight because both Peter and Biffy climbed the steps that led to the slide and then stepped across on to their respective dragon's backs. It was a lot easier than trying to scramble up from the ground. Both the boys were warmed by the dragons before the flight so that they wouldn't feel the incredibly cold air high up in the skies. In actual fact Biffy's clothes were heated up, rather than the boy himself because the magic wouldn't work properly on him. As soon as the scales were locked softly down upon their knees holding them tightly in place, the dragons used their huge wings to lift themselves straight up into the air. Peter looked down and felt excited and scared at the same time, even more so when he saw his home beneath them gradually getting smaller and smaller. They were off on their rescue adventure.

"Has dragon time kicked in now, McDragon?"

"Yes, Petersmith, it actually commenced when you left your house, and it is the same for Master Biffy."

"Thank goodness! I was so worried about leaving home without letting my mum and dad know where I was going."

"As you should be, Petersmith. As you should be."

Peter felt in his pocket and without taking it out he closed his fingers around the small dragon scale that was there.

"How do you do, Spit?" he asked politely once Spit appeared in a picture in his head.

"Very well, thank you Petersmith," and Spit began to giggle. Peter saw that Seraphina and little Popple were close by.

"We are on our way Spit, can you let Seraphina know please?"

"Of course!" Spit looked rather serious for a moment. "Keep safe, Petersmith! I would not like anything bad to happen to you!"

Once he had finished his conversation with Spit, Peter asked McDragon if he should send a message to Brenda. McDragon rather thought that would be a good idea.

The walkie talkies came into use as Peter spoke to Biffy, discussing how best to make Brenda aware of the plan. They sung with gusto the usual tune of Land of Hope and Glory but then changed the words to "We are on our way. Meet us at the plateau." They waited until, out of nowhere, a dragon cloud came towards them. The dragon in the cloud was snorting fire and smiling – in a dragon sort of way – Brenda had most certainly understood their message. Peter had felt McDragon wince as soon as he'd began singing and then again, felt the dragon relax once it was over.

To pass the time on the flight Peter told McDragon all about the new bully gang at school and explained that he felt he should do something about it, but he wasn't sure what. He also told him what Spit had said about not using dragon magic unless it was really needed.

"You have grown, Petersmith. You are most definitely Dragon kin. When we first met you were a rather scared boy and now you have confidence, much like a dragon."

"Thank you, McDragon, that is a really nice thing to say!"

"Young Spit is correct, you will somehow find a solution to your problem, Petersmith. It will come to you."

As they flew high in the clouds Peter gave the matter some thought. He was determined that he would find a way to sort it out one way or another. As he mulled it over, he considered what he thought as the worst part of being bullied – apart from the fear of being physically attacked, for him, the main one had been that he had always felt so alone.

Putting those thoughts aside for the time being he went over his experiment the night before with the wand and the book. When he had touched the wand, he had received a picture of the witch's garden again and he'd tried to force a picture back to Finnia showing the two dragons in flight. There had been no response. Still clutching the magical wand in his dodgy hand, he'd turned the pages of the book until he reached the one with the strange words on it. A faint picture had begun to take shape. As

Peter studied it he could see a sleeve ending in a wide drooping coloured cuff. The purple material had stars on it. A hand holding on to the wand came into his vision – it was pointing at a stone dragon. The whole page began to glow and then the wand in the book moved with a flicking action – the words almost jumped off the page into his head. He heard them clearly in his mind and he mouthed the words silently trying to etch them into his brain. Then blankness returned to the page and to his mind. Although he turned over more pages there was nothing to look at apart from blank yellowing paper.

* * *

The regular movement of the huge wings rocked him to sleep until the crackle and hiss of the walkie talkie in his pocket rudely awakened him.

"Yes, Biffy? Did you want me?" he answered drowsily as he pressed the green speaker button.

"Look down, Dragon boy – you can see the mountains in the distance. We're getting close."

There on the horizon were the snow peaked mountains. Peter shivered – he had to admit he was more than a little scared.

Putting his binoculars to his eyes he studied the mountain peaks ahead of them. McDragon had already told him they would be taking a route that was not directly above the witch's cottage so as not to attract the attention of the gargoyles that might be on guard there.

Again, they sang a song to Brenda, but a very short one much to McDragon's relief, so that she would be aware

156

that they were close by and as they waited for the usual dragon cloud to appear suddenly something red and sleek burst out from behind a passing cloud.

"What ho, Brenda!" Peter shouted to her. He received a dip of her head as a response as the three dragons flew in an arrow formation with Brenda in the lead angling straight for the plateau where she'd first met Peter.

They landed in turn and as soon as Peter was released by the dragon scales and had slipped to the ground he began the dragon greeting hum. All three dragons sang along with him, as did Biffy.

"So, Pedrsmith, I see how you ride a dragon. As I told you before, a Welsh dragon would not allow that to happen!"

A smile crept over Peter's face as McDragon answered, "But, he is Dragon kin and Master Biffy is his assistant and that is very important to us Scottish dragons. They have both played essential roles in serious dragon matters where an evil wizard has been involved."

Straight to the point and to interrupt any discourse over the rights and wrongs of a human riding a dragon Peter asked, "Brenda, do you know where the witch has hidden Finnia?"

"She is in plain sight in the witch's garden – she has been turned to stone."

His heart sank to his boots as he admitted, "I know, it was me that did it."

The red dragon gave him a fierce glare and smoke emitted from her nostrils.

CHAPTER TWENTY-EIGHT

The two boys settled themselves down onto a boulder waiting while Brenda led the dragons to a safe place to fish and drink. They took the time to eat some of the food which Biffy had packed – ham sandwiches and some of the homemade cake. They followed this down with a swig of water.

Biffy rubbed his tummy as he said, "That feels better! I was getting a little hungry up there in the sky. I wonder what time it is at home?"

"It should be the same time as when we left. McDragon told me that dragon time had kicked in immediately we left our houses."

"I wish someone would explain that to my stomach!" Biffy complained, "but at least we shouldn't have to answer any awkward questions when we get back."

"If…" Peter muttered gloomily. He still felt so guilty that he'd had to leave home without telling his parents. He knew it was wrong.

"Chin up, Dragon boy! It is written that you will rescue Finnia, we have to believe that or else we're doomed." Biffy said as he tidied away the remnants of their picnic.

At that very moment they heard the tramp of a pair of boots and the thump of a stick banging on the ground in time with the footsteps.

"Hide! She's coming!"

The pair of them dashed behind the boulder they were sitting on throwing themselves down onto their tummies and slithering further down the hill. The footsteps continued marching past them and up the path. Luckily the sun hadn't risen very high in the sky and they were cloaked in shadow.

Peter's hand gripped Spit's dragon scale and in his head he spoke quickly, "Spit! Warn McDragon not to come back to the plateau! The witch has just gone by up the hill! Did you copy that Spit?"

There was a brief moment's pause and Spit answered very speedily, "Copied Petersmith. I will pass the message on immediately!"

The boys waited for a good few minutes until Biffy suggested that the best option for them would be to go down the path as quickly as they could and get back into the village. They crept along in single file from where they were hiding before joining the track and then broke into run. Even Biffy managed that, which was a real feat for him.

At the bottom he bent over double trying to regain his breath, "Lucky you said to wear trainers rather than wellies!" he panted.

"I wonder what she's doing out this early?" Peter mused aloud. "While she's out let's go take a peek at her cottage and the garden. If we go down this other path we should come out above the back of the garden and high enough for us to use the binoculars. But first, let me tell Spit what we plan to do so he can warn McDragon."

The young dragon answered the summons immediately and as soon as Peter had told him the plan Spit burst into speech in Peter's head.

"Brenda has told McDragon that the garden has magical wards around it to stop intruders getting in. Whatever you do, do *not* step inside the boundary!"

Peter related this to Biffy and then answered Spit. "We will just do a reconnoitre, do you know what that is Spit? It means checking it out. I'll let you know what we see shortly."

"Don't be spotted by the squawkins, Petersmith!"

The boys hunkered down on a ridge behind the house, hiding behind a bush while Peter used the binoculars to gauge how they might be able to get into the garden.

"Finnia is quite near the house," he reported to Biffy, "still as a statue. I wonder how heavy she is? Here you look."

With the binoculars focussed on the garden Biffy swung them from left to right and back again.

"There's a gargoyle sitting right next to her!" he studied the gargoyle some more and added, "But it's not like the other gargoyles, they seem to leer but this one has an ugly but kind face and what's sad about it is that it has a tear drop beneath its eye as if it's crying."

"How very strange. I wish I could speak to Finnia."

"Well you could always try holding the wand like you did before when she sent you that picture. It could be that being closer to her might make a difference. On the other hand, we don't know if the witch will sense it."

"I think I'll take the risk but get ready to run or hide if we need to. See up there, there's a ledge which would hide us from view, we'll go for that if we have to."

Opening his backpack Peter carefully withdrew the wand, at the same time he made sure his jacket was unzipped so he could slide the wand inside if he had to make a speedy escape.

"Can you close up my bag please, so I don't drop anything if we run?"

It was quite difficult trying not to be emotional as he looked down at Finnia's still form, waiting… and waiting.

"Anything?" Biffy asked quietly.

"Not yet, but I've never imagined that wands actually existed before now and I have little idea how to make it work." He squeezed his eyes shut and concentrated as hard as he could focussing totally on Finnia and shutting everything around them out of his head.

A voice whispered rather sweetly in his ear, "Petersmith, I knew you would come!"

"Finnia! Is that you?" Peter answered excitedly.

"It is indeed."

"Thank goodness you can speak to me. We are trying to work out how to get you, but it might be a little harder because of you now being made of stone. I'm so very sorry about that! Can I reverse the magic somehow?"

"Do not fret, Petersmith, because you altered me the witch has been unable to use me for her nefarious purposes, and she has tried and tried. You *know* how to bring me alive and young Biffy is the key to getting past her wards. Use him. I will be able to help if you can change me back from stone but lastly and, most importantly you need to bring Aloysius alive too and then take him with us!"

"Who?" Peter almost shouted in his surprise.

"The gargoyle who is next to me – he is a friend and… probably the last true descendant of the first gargoyles, as I too, may be the last of my kind. He will be needed in things to come."

"O…Okay!"

"Go now, Petersmith! She nears us!"

Peter grabbed at Biffy and whispered, "Hide!"

CHAPTER TWENTY-NINE

It seemed strange to think that they had only been in the village for a very short time but that so much had already happened. It had thrown them completely when they realised the witch was out and about so very early in the day. Thankfully, due to Finnia's warning the witch hadn't noticed Biffy and Peter in their hideaway above the garden and once she'd gone into her cottage they were able to shoot back up the path to meet McDragon, Haribald and Brenda at the plateau.

Peter puzzled over his conversation with Finnia.

"So, Biffy is the key to the gate... What do you think that means, McDragon?"

It was actually Biffy who answered, "I think it could well be that because I am non-magical I might be able to pass through the wards without them affecting me."

Rather downcast, Peter told the dragons about Finnia insisting that they save Aloysius too and why.

"Oh, and I didn't have time to tell you that when I was studying the wizard's book there was a picture showing him magicking a stone dragon to life – the only trouble is I've now forgotten the words he used! I've tried and tried to remember them. How could I possibly forget something that is so important!" Peter responded rather gloomily. "Are we doomed on this mission?!"

"Have some cake, Dragon boy. Food always helps me perk up a bit, so maybe it'll do the same for you too – takes your mind off things." Biffy said as he thrust a piece of cake at his friend. Food was Biffy's answer to everything and to keep the peace Peter took it and bit rather absentmindedly into it.

"I really think your brain is in your stomach Biffy!" Peter muttered with his mouth full. He savoured the sweetness of the food in his mouth while he chewed thoughtfully for a while.

"Perhaps you will remember when you use the wand for the purpose you have brought it for, Petersmith," Haribald suggested sagely.

Peter fingered the wand absentmindedly in his hands – he didn't even remember picking it up and he was shocked when Finnia's voice came across to him again.

"She is leaving so now would be a good time to come! But mind – the guards are at the front door, so beware!"

* * *

Following the plan that they'd made during their pow wow Brenda took off to draw any possible pursuers away from them. The boys scampered back down the path towards the back of the house, the dragons soaring high overhead, ready to dive down and give assistance if needed.

Wand clutched in his good hand, Peter followed Biffy down the side of the back garden, both of them trying to keep their heads below the fence line. It was very squelchy underfoot, so it must have rained a lot recently. Reaching the gate Biffy poked his head around the side, doing a careful reccy.

He turned back towards Peter and whispered, "All seems OK. I'm going in!"

They'd arranged that Biffy would enter first with Peter pressed up against him so that maybe, just maybe, they could go through the gate together without triggering an alarm. Peter tugged on Biffy's arm stopping him and pointed down to their shoes. He handed Biffy a big dock leaf indicating that he should wipe off the mud which had accumulated on his trainers, Peter doing the same. It would be dangerous enough as it was without adding the chance of slipping to the task. Job done they then began to carefully proceed.

Peter made sure that when Biffy put a foot forward, he mirrored him so that their feet touched the ground at the same time. It was a very slow business. One foot after the other was placed down carefully on the random paving stones that made up the path, then another and another and they were through. Phew!

Scanning the area Peter saw the gargoyle, Aloysius staring straight at them. He looked rather scary, but his mouth was up on one side as if he was giving them a very peculiar smile and the tear drop on his cheek had disappeared without a trace. How weird was that?!

Peter held the wand high, ready to do the necessary flick at Finnia but as he tried to move his hand he found he was frozen in place – he couldn't move!

A loud cackle sounded from behind the house and then the witch appeared, clad in her red cloak as usual and the black beret perched on top of her head. Her eyes gleamed evilly in delight as she raised her walking stick to point it at Peter.

"Ha! Ha! I sensed that you had come!" she shrieked, "I will have that wand – it will be of great use to me!" As she spoke two squawkins hurtled from around the corner, uttering their ear-splitting screeches.

Still frozen, Peter desperately wanted to run, he was quaking right down to the depths of his core. He stared at Finnia, but there was no hope in that direction, she was as still as the stone she had become. Above the house he could see a big red dragon arrowing towards them, but she was much too far away to help. McDragon and Haribald d'Ness too were flying as fast as they could behind her.

The witch opened her mouth and began hissing some unintelligible magical words, just as at that very moment Biffy flung himself between her and Peter. The magic from her walking stick hit into him slamming him to the ground with a huge thud, but his actions released Peter from his frozen state and he flourished the wand in the air pointing it directly at Finnia – the words he had forgotten flew out of his mouth and sparks jettisoned from the wand blasting into her. He then turned to Aloysius and the identical words magically came from his mouth as the same multi-coloured sparks burst against the gargoyle.

The cloaked woman screamed, her long droopy nose turning red in anger.

Both Finnia and Aloysius came to life, fire bursting from Finnia's open maw straight at the witch's walking stick turning it to ash in her hand.

Another shriek came from the witch's open mouth as she stared at the grey mound which was beginning to scatter on the breeze.

"No..ooo!"

Finnia turned her attention to the stone dragons which were resting along the edge of the garden up one side of the patchy grass. She almost floated up from the ground on very delicate wings and flew elegantly across to the dragons blowing fire into each of their faces, one at a time. Immediately the flames hit them the dragons leapt into life and circled the witch bowling her down onto the ground.

Amazingly, Aloysius was more than a match for the squawkins, all he had to do was raise one long spindly finger and point it at their enemy who froze in the air and crashed down onto the path, smashing into hundreds of tiny pieces.

Biffy remained motionless on the ground and Peter rushed over to him, slapping his face trying to bring him round. No movement at all so he pressed his ear against his friend's chest trying to hear his heart.

"No!…" he shouted, tears streaming down his face. "No!!!"

A small scaled creature landed lightly on Peter's shoulders and a long tail wrapped around his neck, a soft nose touching his cheek, as if in a kiss before Finnia leapt onto the still body of the boy flat on the ground. She pushed Peter's head out of the way and pressed her nose against Biffy's nose snorting steam rather than fire into his nostrils. Biffy's chest remained motionless. Aloysius shuffled to stand next to her and pointed his index finger at Biffy, flicking it very gently at the boy's chest. Sparks shot out from his long nail and hit Biffy's chest. Peter held his breath waiting and waiting. Tears continued to stream down his face and all he could think about was how on earth was he going to explain to Biffy's parents what had happened and how very much he would miss his friend.

Suddenly Biffy's whole body shuddered and his rib cage began to rise and fall unevenly until it finally settled back into a steady rhythm.

"Thank goodness!" Peter muttered as the bigger lad pushed himself into a sitting position.

"What happened there?" he asked groggily, shaking his head from side to side.

"Are you OK" Peter asked holding tightly onto Biffy's arm.

"I…I think so! I thought I had died!"

"I thought that as well! Finnia and Aloysius did something to you to bring you back."

"Thank you, Finnia! Thank you, Aloysius!" Biffy bowed his head to the tiny dragona and gargoyle as Finnia pressed her nose gently against him in response.

Biffy added, "I'm going to make a special cake for you both to show you how happy I am that you managed to bring me back to life." Peter just had to smile at that.

"Petersmith – we must leave immediately before the stone dragons are drained of the magic I gave them. The witch will be dangerous when she comes to, even without her magic walking stick. Please can you ask Master Biffy to pick up Aloysius and bring him with us – his wings haven't formed yet."

As time was of the essence Peter, rather sensibly, didn't question how Finnia could now communicate with him so easily – no doubt he would find out at some point in the future.

He used Spit's scale to ask him to issue instructions to the big dragons and then he passed on Finnia's message to Biffy. The big boy was standing and staring curiously at the gargoyle – the gargoyle returned his gaze for a few moments before Biffy's feet took him towards the small creature and he put his hands down and swept him up pushing him gently inside his jacket.

CHAPTER THIRTY

Back at the plateau Brenda landed lightly beside the two other dragons. The boys were standing next to them, Finnia wrapped around Peter's neck and Aloysius' head peeking out from the security of Biffy's jacket.

Brenda explained how the witch had managed to appear without any warning. Brenda had been caught out by a surprise attack from the witch's two squawkins. who had appeared from nowhere and once she had fought them off it was too late, the witch had already returned to her cottage.

"It doesn't matter Brenda! All's well that ends well! That's another one of my mum's sayings. After all, it did help us in a way because the squawkins couldn't be in two places at once, it meant they were not at the cottage to see us enter the garden."

"Well said, Petersmith!" McDragon's voice boomed out. "We must be away Brenda, but it is very good that we Scottish dragons have now met a Welsh one! You are welcome to visit us on the Isle of Harris anytime you see fit – it would be a pleasure to introduce you to Seer Effel, Seraphina and the young ones, Spit and little Popple."

Brenda bowed her head regally in agreement, as Finnia flew from Peter's shoulders and landed on a boulder close to Brenda. The big red dragon and the minute lumescent grey one touched their noses, to commune with one another.

"I believe we will meet again, Petersmith." Brenda announced, "My thanks go with you for rescuing Finnia. I still find it strange that a human, and in fact, an English one, was the key to her rescue. However, do be aware that she is important to all dragon kind be it Welsh, Scottish or any other. Also, do remember that the witch will be relentless in her pursuit and will try her utmost to recapture her. Somehow, and I know not how, she has found out that Finnia is an incredibly special dragona and what's more, she will now have a great interest in Aloysius. You *must* be on your guard at all times!"

She turned to Biffy, "You were magnificent, Master Biffy. You should be very proud of yourself."

"I agree," Peter interrupted earning himself a glare from the proud Welsh dragon, but he saw that Biffy was beaming from ear to ear.

After being warmed, the boys were helped getting aboard their mounts by the dragons pushing them up with their snouts. Aloysius looking quite content in where he was with Biffy.

"I still do not believe a Welsh dragon would allow a human boy to ride it!" Brenda announced.

"Each to his own!" Peter smiled back at her, "That's another one of my mum's sayings. She has a lot of them."

Once the scales had locked into place over his knees Finnia spread her wings and flew to land gently on his shoulder and he opened his jacket to enable her to slip inside.

The sun still hadn't risen very high in the sky on their return journey home. Brenda accompanied them part of the way before dipping her wings and beginning her flight back to the mountains. They had agreed before leaving that the boys would continue to sing messages to her, keeping her in touch with what was happening with Finnia.

"Well, that was certainly different," Peter murmured to McDragon. He was too buoyed up with adrenaline to be able to doze.

"It was at that, Petersmith. Without young Biffy I do not believe you could have managed the rescue – he took his life in his hands putting himself between you and the witch's spell."

"He was amazing, wasn't he? I thought he'd died!"

"I believe he may have done just that but the combined magic of Finnia and Aloysius brought him back to life. He is a very lucky young man!"

McDragon had already updated Seraphina and Spit via the scale but Peter still spoke to his dragon friend filling him in on the extra details until, with Finnia dozing happily against him, the tension gradually began to leave his body.

He allowed various thoughts to run through his head before he finally nodded off. He knew he would need to rest because, ridiculously, he had to go to school as soon as he got back. How on earth could life carry on normally after such an adventure?

* * *

The dragons landed in the park next to the swings and slide where they had first met the boys. Once the scales had released him Peter slid to the ground and opened his jacket to allow Finnia to clamber out of his coat – he felt sure she would return to the Isle of Harris with McDragon.

"Oh no, Petersmith. I wish to remain with you!" she announced in his head, "McDragon is aware that that is what I desire to happen."

"But… will you be safe with me? I would rather you were not at risk. I am just a small boy, in fact one of the smallest in my year at school!"

"Petersmith, you may be little, but you have a big heart and that is what counts for more than size. I am an Elfinn dragona and, I too am very small, but I was brought into being to be with a wizard. You are my wizard of choice, Petersmith!"

"I'm not a wizard!"

"You are indeed – you are the keeper of the wand and the magical book. That is the reason I am now able to speak to you mind to mind. Trust me, that is how it should be!"

"I am honoured, Finnia, truly honoured that you wish to remain with me. I will try not to let you down." He spoke the words aloud so that McDragon, Haribald and Biffy could hear them.

"That you could never do – you are truly Dragon kin!" McDragon told him.

It was sad to see the dragons disappear over the horizon. McDragon had kept Seraphina's scale for the time being but promised to return it to Peter on his next visit to the Isle of Harris. That wasn't too far in the future seeing as the whole Smith family would be travelling up there for the summer holidays, Biffy included.

It seemed rather ridiculous that Peter met Biffy at the corner at their usual time so that they could walk to school together. Both of them were rather shocked when they thought back to their adventure and the rescue of Finnia. It seemed rather weird to be so normal again. Aloysius, too, had opted to remain with the boys but he preferred to be out in the open air and therefore was settled comfortably at the bottom of Biffy's small garden. No-one ever went down there apparently, so it was totally overgrown. Neither of the lads had any idea of what his purpose was to be, but Finnia had said he was important and they believed her.

Peter had left the tiny dragona snoozing in his bedroom, keeping guard over the wizard's book and the wand.

At the school gates they saw the bullies waiting, but they were both relieved that just as they approached it seemed that they were not the prey today. The gang surrounded one of the other boys in front of them and hustled him along.

Clutching Spit's scale in his hand so that Spit could hear him, Peter said quietly to his friend, "Biffy, I know what I wish to do for the bullied children – I gave it much thought on the flight there and back."

"What do you want to do, Dragon boy?"

"I remember what for me was the very worst part of being bullied," and Biffy had the grace to look ashamed. "And that was the feeling of being so alone. We can help with that."

"Can we? How?"

"We will form a secret group called "The Dragon Society". We cannot fight the bullies because that'll make us as bad as them, but maybe we can offer friendship to those that need our help so that they feel they are not alone. We'll have to make a plan." Biffy was quiet as he mulled that over, but Spit said delightedly through the dragon scale, "You are proving yourself to be Dragon kin yet again, Petersmith! Most definitely, Dragon kin! The dragons chose well. Over and Out!"

Peter's beam said it all.

After walking in silence for a while he spluttered with laughter as he suddenly heard Biffy murmur, "I wonder if my parents would eat Cullen Skink?"

NOTE FROM THE AUTHOR

I hope you enjoyed reading "McFinnia" and if you have time please could you put a review on Amazon or my Facebook page about it. A good review encourages other people to buy it.

A tiny taster of the fourth book in the "McDragon" series which is called "McRumble" is on the next page.

CHAPTER ONE

He was running out of puff and it was only sheer determination that was keeping him above the rippling waves. He knew that he was very close to crashing into the sea where he would sink very slowly to the bottom and never be seen again. His wings felt like they were lead weights and it was getting harder and harder to move them up and down to keep him aloft. He just had to reach Petersmith! He just had to be in time to protect his best friend from the danger that was stalking him. The friend who was also Dragon kin. He had to keep going somehow! His scaled belly skimmed the top of the water... oh no, was this nearly the end?!

To make sure you buy a copy of "McRumble" as soon as it is available please follow me on my facebook page:

Pamghoward@pamghowardchildrensbooks

or on my website:

https://www.pamghowardchildrensbooks.com

or on Instagram
pamghowardauthor